·中华文化研究丛刊·

汉英元曲赏析

耿娟

著

九州出版社
JIUZHOUPRESS

图书在版编目（CIP）数据

汉英元曲赏析／耿娟著 . --北京：九州出版社，
2024.1

　　ISBN 978－7－5225－2556－3

　　Ⅰ.①汉… Ⅱ.①耿… Ⅲ.①元曲—文学欣赏—英文
Ⅳ.①I207.24

中国国家版本馆 CIP 数据核字（2024）第 034003 号

汉英元曲赏析

作　　者	耿　娟　著	
责任编辑	蒋运华	
出版发行	九州出版社	
地　　址	北京市西城区阜外大街甲 35 号（100037）	
发行电话	（010）68992190/3/5/6	
网　　址	www. jiuzhoupress. com	
印　　刷	唐山才智印刷有限公司	
开　　本	710 毫米×1000 毫米　16 开	
印　　张	11.5	
字　　数	143 千字	
版　　次	2024 年 1 月第 1 版	
印　　次	2024 年 1 月第 1 次印刷	
书　　号	ISBN 978－7－5225－2556－3	
定　　价	85.00 元	

序

所谓元曲，包含着两种不同体裁的艺术，一为杂剧，属戏剧艺术的范畴；一为散曲，是金元时期发展起来的一种独具特色的抒情诗。散曲又可分小令、带过曲、套曲三类。当然，两者之间也存在着相当紧密的联系，散曲和杂剧中的唱词使用着同样的格律形式，就是在思想倾向、语言风格上，两者也保持着一致。

从现存作品看，散曲表现的思想内容主要集中于两个方面，一为市井山林隐逸之思，另一则是对男女风情的表现。就艺术形式而言，散曲与词一样，原属音乐文学的范畴，但在长期的发展流传中，其文学的一面获得了自足的价值。但总体来说，散曲艺术始终未能尽掩其民间本色。在意美方面，散曲使诗歌更加大众化；在音美方面，散曲使韵律更加自由化；在形美方面，散曲使格式更加多样化。总而言之，元曲把诗歌进一步推向通俗化、口语化、灵活化，成为大众更加喜闻乐见的文学形式。

优秀传统文化的魅力，归根结底在于它扎根人民的生命深处，与人民的生活融为一体，从而让我们对于优秀传统文化充满了自信和自豪。这本书的翻译，也是源于上述原因，并且希望让更多的国际友人了解中国优秀传统文化，让中国优秀传统文化同世界各国优秀文化一道造福人类。

　　本书得到邵宁宁教授的授权，同意将其《元曲品读》著作中的45首品读文字部分进行翻译；对元曲古文的翻译借鉴了许渊冲先生《元曲三百首》译著的许多思想，在这里再次表达对二位的感谢之情！

目　录
CONTENTS

人月圆
卜居外家东园
元好问

重冈已隔红尘断，

村落更年丰。

移居要就，

窗中远岫，

舍后长松。

十年种木，

一年种谷，

都付儿童。

老夫惟有，

醒来明月，

醉后清风。

品读

这首小令，先描述自己"卜居外家"后远离城市，与山林为伴的生活，后则直接叙写在新环境中的平民生活。虽然由于作者年事已高，体力不济，致使"十年种木，一年种谷，都付儿童"，但是却充满着一种心理上的满足，一种与"明月""清风"相处的和谐与美感。字里行间，蕴含着对当朝统治者的不满情绪，可谓绵里藏针。在写作手法上，对偶工整，骈散结合，节奏铿锵，毫不板滞。

Tune：Man and Moon

Moving to My Mother's East Garden

Yuan Haowen

Hill on hill keeps apart the vanity of the world,

From this village of a good harvest year.

I move to come near.

From window you can see the distant hill,

And behind the windowsill the pine-trees.

I'll leave the trees and fields

To the hands of my kins.

So that, I can do what I will.

I'll enjoy the moon so bright after awakening,

And the refreshing breeze so gentle after drinking.

Literary Appreciation

This song poem first describes the life the speaker led, residing amidst mountains, after moving from the city to the home of the speaker's mother, and then directly narrates the civilian life within this new environment. Despite the speaker's old age and physical weakness, which leads to "I'll leave the trees and fields to the hands of my kins", they achieved a profound sense of psychological satisfaction, with harmonious and aesthetic appreciation for the "bright moon" and the "gentle breeze." Implicit in the lines is a sense of discontent towards the ruler of their current dynasty, akin to an iron fist in a velvet glove. In terms of writing techniques, the writer skillfully utilized antithesis and combined parallel prose and free prose, giving the song poem a sonorous rhythm.

干荷叶

刘秉忠

干荷叶，

色苍苍，

老柄风摇荡。

减了清香，

越添黄。

都因昨夜一场霜，

寂寞在秋江上。

品读

这是刘秉忠小令《干荷叶》八首中传诵最广最具代表性的一首。作品开门见山，起头便点出"干荷叶"，并描绘其色彩的浅淡和只剩一"老柄"时的凄凉孤单，接着抒发干荷叶因遭严霜而枯槁寂寞的情景。通篇字数不多，却流畅自然，极富民歌气息。细加品读，似乎在咏物中暗寓着一种失意和潦倒，显得别具韵味。

Tune: Dried Lotus Leaves

Liu Bingzhong

Lotus leaves dried.

Their color turned from green to withered and yellow.

Their old stems swayed in the wind.

Because of the yellow dye, they lost fragrance.

Frost last night chilled their dream.

Now they look lonely on the autumn stream.

Literary Appreciation

This is the most representative song poem among the total eight*Dried Lotus Leaves* by Liu Bingzhong. This work comes straight to the point, beginning with the "dried lotus leaves", depicting their colors and the sense of desolation and solitude when only one "old stem" remains. Then, it portrays a solitary scene of the withered lotus leaves because of the harsh frost. Although concise, this work is smooth and natural, replete with the essence of folk songs. Upon closer review, it becomes evident that the passage conveys a hidden meaning that suggests both frustration and confusion, which is a combination of emotions with unique charm.

节节高

题洞庭鹿角庙壁

卢挚

雨晴云散，

满江明月。

风微浪息，

扁舟一叶。

半夜心，

三生梦，

万里别，

闷倚篷窗睡些。

品读

洞庭鹿角庙，未详。这首小令，前四句分别描写雨云、江月、风浪、扁舟之景，展现出一片安详宁静气象，反映出作者生活的平静舒适和内心的安然和谐。后四句则写作者的情绪低沉和清闲无聊。以"半夜心""三生梦""万里别"连续突出心理的孤寂，一个"闷倚篷窗睡些"的动作加上无奈的语调，顿使环境冷漠凄清，人物孤苦孑立、形影相吊，生动而深刻地抒发出当时生活于社会底层的知识分子的空虚和苦闷。景虽简淡，情却深长。

Tune: Higher and Higher

Written on the wall of Lujiao Temple on Lake Dongting

Lu Zhi

The clouds clear away after the rain,

The moon cast a bright light over the lake.

The waves are calm when the wind is light,

And a leaf boat is seen at midnight.

From the bottom of my heart,

Of my past life I dream.

To a distant land I'll go,

Dispirited in the lonesome boat, I'll rest a slumber brief.

Literary Appreciation

Lujiao Temple on the Dongting Lake, undetailed. The first four sentences of this song poem each describes the imagery of rain and clouds, water and moon, winds and waves, and boats, conveying a serene and tranquil ambiance, reflecting the speaker's calm and comfortable life, as well as their inner peace and harmony. Meanwhile, the latter four sentences show a tone characterized by feelings of sadness and languor. The theme of psychological loneliness is consistently highlighted through phrases such as "the bottom of my heart," "past life I dream," and "to a distant land I'll go." The action of the speaker, who is described as being "dispirited in the lonesome boat" and taking "a slumber brief," contributes to the overall sense of helplessness, creating a cold and desolate environment, in which the speaker stood alone. This work vividly and profoundly expresses the emptiness and depression experienced by intellectuals living at the lower echelons of society during that era. Despite the simplicity of the scenary described, it has a profound and long-lasting emotional impact.

四块玉
别情
关汉卿

自送别，

心难舍，

一点相思几时绝？

凭阑袖拂杨花雪。

溪又斜，

山又遮，

人去也。

品读

这首小令抒发一位思妇倚楼而望，想念远方心上人的心情。全曲以思妇口吻，先叙离别之情一直未断，后述对心上人思念之切，同时以袖拂杨花这一动作，细腻刻画怨妇望眼欲穿、久立寒风之中的心态，描写生动传神。再衬以山高水长，将思情之深长悠远表现得具体细微，言已尽而意无穷，韵调耐人寻味。

Tune: Four Pieces of Jade

Parting Grief

Guan Hanqing

Since you have left,

I take you to my heart and soul.

When will my ache for you find its end?

Leaning on rails, snow-like plum blossom wiped away with my sleeves.

The winding stream,

The rolling hills.

The views remind me so much that,

You have left.

Literary Appreciation

This song poem describes the emotions experienced by a woman that leans against a pavilion while reminiscing about her distant loved ones. The entirety of the song poem adopts a tone that reflects the sentiment of the woman, first recounting her emotions due to the partings, which have yet to subside, then vividly depicting the strong feelings experienced when missing her loved ones. At the same time, the act of brushing the snow off with her sleeves thoroughly and vividly portrays the emotional state of the upset woman who is eager to reunite and willing to stand in the cold wind for an extended period. The soulful emotions of longing are also eloquently and subtlety conveyed through descriptions of high mountains and waters. The emotions experienced are beyond the limitations of words, leading to the captivating combination of rhyme and tune in this song poem.

四块玉

闲适

关汉卿

（一）

意马收，

心猿锁，

跳出红尘恶风波。

槐荫午梦谁惊破？

离了利名场，

钻入安乐窝，

闲快活！

（二）

南亩耕，

东山卧，

世态人情经历多。

闲将往事思量过。

贤的是他，

愚的是我，

争甚么？

品读

这两首小令写对现实的不满，表达了一种绝意仕进、与世无争的逃避情绪，流露出对世事的一种忧愤和不平。第一首写作者逃脱名利场后的闲适快活心情，充满着他对"红尘"的深恶痛绝和对功名富贵、荣华利禄无常的体验，也间接抒发了作者对宦海风波的超脱，在一种回避的心态中隐藏着对现实社会的不满。第二首则直言隐退田园的快乐心情。作者回忆往事，百感交集，不平和愤慨之情顿时涌上心头，继而又以"贤的是他，愚的是我，争甚么"的愤世之语，点名退隐的最大原因，同时也表现出对世间混淆黑白、颠倒是非、不分贤愚状况的忧愤和不满。

Tune: Four Pieces of Jade

Leisure Life

Guan Hanqing

(I)

Whimsical mind now closed,

Empty heart now dead,

Leap from the world which raves with dust and waves.

Awake from empty daydreams of vain glory!

Get away from fame and gain.

Rest in the nest of pleasure.

And enjoy your life!

(II)

Plough the soil of southern fields,

And reside by the eastern hill's foot.

I've known the world and its ways,

Remembered so many things of the past days.

How wise he is,

And how foolish I am!

What should I contend to be?

Literary Appreciation

These two song poems convey a sense of discontent towards reality, while also expressing a determination to progress and escape from the world, and exuding anger towards the world. The first song poem captures a sense of leisure and contentment following the speaker's separation from the vanity fair, and the deep hatred of "the world which raves with dust and waves" and their experience of capricious fame and wealth. Indirectly, it also conveys the speaker's detachment from the tumultuous affairs of theofficialdom, evasively hiding their dissatisfaction with the real world. The second song poem is a straightforward depiction of the joyful sentiment experienced when retiring to the countryside. The speaker recalled the past, which stirred a combination of emotions, including a sense of injustice and indignation that suddenly welled up. Then, through "How wise he is, And how foolish I am! What should I contend to be?" the writer highlighted the primary factor behind the speaker's decision to retire while simultaneously expressing their frustration and discontent with the state of affairs in the world, where values are distorted, right and wrong are reversed, and the ability to differentiate between wisdom and foolishness is absent.

沉醉东风
送别
关汉卿

咫尺的天南地北，
霎时间月缺花飞。
手执着饯行杯，
眼阁着别离泪。
刚道得声保重将息，
痛煞煞叫人舍不得。
好去者，
望前程万里！

品读

这是一首饯别之作。作者先以"天南地北""月缺花飞"极言离别之苦，继而描画分别之景，以手执饯行酒杯、眼含别离情泪两个细节，一描外在动态，一写内在心理。虽然分手在即，二人不愿分开，但主人公还是殷勤寄语，祝愿行者能一路平安、保重自己，言语未终而心痛欲绝，写出了两人之间的深情厚谊。最后又一次叮咛嘱咐，希望行者前程万里、一帆风顺，再次表达出对别离之人的诚挚祝福。全曲描景抒情细腻生动，真切感人，悲中含喜，具有独特的格调和魅力。

Tune: Indulged in East Wind

Farewell Song

Guan Hanqing

Close we were, soon apart;

At this moment, flowers fall, and moon dims.

In our hands, the parting glass we hold.

Our eyes brim with tears.

"Take care and keep in touch!"

My throat choked and my heart hurt.

To tear myself away!

I can only say, "Go forth, with my best wishes!"

Literary Appreciation

This is asong poem centered about the theme of farewell. At first, the writer expressed the bitterness of parting, as evident in the sentences "close we were, soon apart" and "flowers fall, and moon dims". Then, he painted the scene of parting by highlighting two specific elements: holding a parting glass and eyes brimming with tears, through which he captured both the external dynamics and the internal psychological state of both the speaker and the other party. Despite their impending separation, both are reluctant to separate. Nevertheless, the speaker expresses their genuine wishes for the other party's safe journey and well-being, which resulted in emotional distress for the speaker before they could finish their sentences, underscoring the deep connection of friendship between the two. Then, the speaker reiterates their well wishes to the leaving party for a bright future and smooth sailing. This song poem portrays various scenes using eloquent and vivid lyricism, skillfully capturing both genuine and heartbreaking emotions and incorporating elements of sadness and joy; these characteristics lend a unique style and charm to the song poem.

碧玉箫

关汉卿

（一）

席上樽前，

衾枕奈无缘。

柳底花边，

诗曲已多年。

向人前未敢言，

自心中祷告天。

情意坚，每日空相见。

天！

甚时节成姻眷？

（二）

膝上琴横，

哀愁动离情。

指下风生，

潇洒弄清声。

锁窗前月色明，

雕阑外夜气清。

指法轻，助起骚人兴。

听！

正漏断人初静。

品读

这两首小令一写相思，一写抚琴，各尽其致。第一首描写一位女子坠入情网，暗中爱上一个男子，但又害羞而不敢告诉他人，所以只好深藏心底，希望老天能保佑她与意中人结好姻缘。全曲描摹女子热烈而又含蓄的爱恋心理，细腻入微，生动逼真。语言上直抒心胸，情感上意志坚定，既具有形象感，显出人物个性，又暗含一种相思之苦的倾诉，委婉深情而又大胆活泼。第二首则以抚琴之景来表达人物之情。全曲既展示了主人公琴艺之娴熟、琴声之美妙及其抚琴环境之幽雅，又抒发了她内心的别离之情和诗人之兴，以音传情，以景衬情，孤独哀怨之情溢于字里行间。此曲描写寂静的环境甚为出色，以"清声""月色明""夜气清""正漏断""人初静"等极力渲染人物所处的情境，再加之哀怨的琴声，更衬托出抚琴者内心的凄楚与荒凉，情景交融、人琴一体，更显悱恻动人。

Tune: Green Jade Flute

Guan Hanqing

(I)

Guqin on my knees,

My distant lover in my thoughts.

Fingers on the strings,

At ease I am to the tune of *guqin*.

Moon shines bright through my window screen,

Fresh night air beyond the balustrade.

Strings played gentle,

The music make the poets lots of fun.

Listen!

Silencereigns,

In the depths of night.

(II)

At the banquet, before a glass of wine,

Beside the flowers, beneath the willow,

For years I've sung and you've written verse divine,

But no chance to share, the quilt and pillow.

What before all others I dare to speak?

In my heart I can only pray.

Although our love steadfast and true,

Yet day by day we remain apart.

Oh, God,

When shall we wed, in this journey we tread?

21

Literary Appreciation

These two song poems each dedicated to a different theme while exhibiting exemplary qualities in their respective ways; one delves into the art of playing the*guqin*, whereas the other explores lovesickness. The first poem expresses the emotions of the speaker through a scene depicting them playing the *guqin*. It not only showcases her adeptness in playing the *guqin* in a sophisticated environment, which produces melodious tones, but also highlights her emotions aroused from separation, and her desire to create poetry. The writer effectively conveyed the speaker's emotions through sounds and sceneries, as her sentiments of aloneness and sorrow overflow the lines. He also skillfully described the tranquil atmosphere, depicting a scenario in which the speaker stands "at ease" with "the tune of *guqin*," "bright moon," "fresh night air," "silence reigns," and "the depths of night." In addition, the melancholic resonance of the *guqin* amplifies the aloneness and sorrow of the speaker, while the fusion of emotions and sceneries, as well as the seamless integration of the *guqin* and its player, imbue the song poem with a heightened sentiment and emotional impact. The second song—poem describes a scenario wherein a woman has secretly fallen in love with a man, but she harbors these emotions deep within her heart because of her shyness. She asks for a miracle from God that would allow her to unite in matrimony with her lover. This song poem intricately and vividly portrays the psychology of a woman's passionate and implicit love with direct language and resolute willpower. This song poem not only exhibits a vivid imagery that portrays the personalities of the speaker, but also subtly conveys the theme of lovesickness. It is tactful, affectionate, bold, and dynamic.

寄生草

饮

白朴

长醉后方何碍，

不醒时有甚思。

糟腌两个功名字，

醅渰千古兴亡事，

曲埋万丈虹蜺志。

不达时皆笑屈原非。

但知音尽说陶潜是。

品读

　　这首小令通过对饮酒行为的描写，抒发作者对社会现实的强烈不满，同时也反映出其内心的苦闷和抑郁。曲作先以两句牢骚语开头，将屈原"举世皆浊我独清，世人皆醉我独醒"（《渔父》）与李白"钟鼓馔玉不足贵，但愿长醉不复醒"（《将进酒》）之诗意融合，表达出一种愤世嫉俗的情感倾向。继而以饮酒可以忘却功名、历史和理想，极写内心的苦闷之情和以酒浇愁忘忧的痛苦生活。曲终以屈原和陶潜两位古人作结，更觉含蓄蕴藉，绵里藏针。屈原忠心耿耿，愤投汨罗，但很多人都认为他不识时务；陶潜逃避现实，隐居田园，却得到了后人的尊敬，被誉为"古今隐逸诗人之宗"。作者虽表面上以陶潜为知音，认为他做得正确，但骨子里却隐含着一种对政治无道的谴责和对现实黑暗的抨击。虽然这种感情表现得较为微妙而曲折，藏锋未露，但其深层的含义却是不难窥破的。

Tune: Parasitic Grass

Drinking

◆   *Bai Pu*

What hinders my way if I'm long drunk?

What thoughts arise if I don't wake?

In the wine let undying fame and glory drown!

The ebb and flow of days bygone left behind!

In my melody, my great ambitions lie!

Ignorants mock Qu Yuan's end,

While enthusiasts praise Tao Qian's retreat a rightful aim.

Literary Appreciation

Through the depiction of drinking behavior, this song poem expresses the author's strong dissatisfaction with societal norms, while serving as a reflection of his inner anguish and despondency. It begins with two complaints, combining Qu Yuan's poetic expression of "The entire world is corrupt and I am clean alone; everyone is drunk while I am sober alone" in *The Fisherman* with Li Bai's poetic sentiment of "What difference will rare and costly dishes make? I only want to get drunk and never to wake" in the *Invitation to Wine*, conveying cynical emotions. The speaker then resorted to alcohol as a means of escaping from the fame, the past, and personal ideals, which perfectly described their anguish and their drinking behavior as a coping mechanism to escape the hardships endured. The song poem concludes with the mention of Qu Yuan and Tao Qian from the earlier dynasties, adding a sense of subtlety, akin to an iron fist in a velvet glove. Qu Yuan was known for his loyalty and devotion, but many believed that he lacked awareness of current affairs. On the other hand, Tao Qian chose to detach himself from the realities of society and lived in the countryside, but he garnered respect from future generations and earned the title of the "ancestor of ancient and modern recluse poets". While the author outwardly portrays Tao Qian as a close companion and believed his actions to be commendable, there is an underlying disapproval of political immorality and a critique of the harshness of reality. Despite its subtlety and intricate nature, this sentiment harbors a brilliant intellect that can be easily made out due to its profound significance.

天净沙
白朴

（一）春

春山暖日和风，

阑干楼台帘栊，

杨柳秋千院中。

啼莺舞燕，

小桥流水飞红。

（二）夏

云收雨过波添，

楼高水冷瓜甜，

绿树阴垂画檐。

纱幮藤簟，

玉人罗扇轻缣。

（三）秋

孤村落日残霞，

轻烟老树寒鸦，

一点飞鸿影下。

青山绿水，

白草红叶黄花。

（四）冬

一声画角樵门，

半庭新月黄昏，

雪里山前水滨。

竹篱茅舍，

淡烟衰草孤村。

品读

这四首小令分咏春、夏、秋、冬四季景色，写得清丽天然，语言简约。第一首描绘春天风和日暖、万物勃发、山清水秀、莺歌燕舞的如画景致；第二首展现盛夏雨过天晴、碧空如洗，人们悠闲纳凉的情景；第三首描摹秋天萧瑟冷落的景象，又增之以怀人相思之情，堪与马致远《天净沙·秋思》比肩；第四首渲染出一幅悲凉昏暗的冬日晚景图，"一声画角"更使这种情景显得凄壮哀伤。总体看来，通篇写景都很成功，都能紧扣季节的特征来描写，同时以景传情，以情绘景，动静结合，自然天成。尤其是全曲在组成景色画面方面，纯用名词加以白描，虽无动词，却能以静显动，以物传神，质朴清丽，层次鲜明，读来赏心悦目，余味无穷。

Tune: Sunny Sand

Bai Pu

(I) Spring

Gentle winds and warm sunshine in spring's embrace,

The curtained bower girt by balustrade,

Among willows in the garden the swing sways.

The swallows dance and orioles sing,

On running stream under the bridge's shade, reds fade.

(II) Summer

Waves rise and clouds clear when summer storm fades,

Tower high, watermelon's sweet, cold water's feat.

Willow leaves green and bright shade the painted eaves.

A beauty rests on a bed adorned with hanging vine,

In silken dress, brocade fan in hand.

(III) Autumn

Autumn's sunset casts darken glowover the lonely village,

Over mist-veiled old trees a crow soars,

A wild goose glides, its shadow a graceful sight.

Over green hills andclear rills,

Seesleaves red, flowers yellow, and dewy grass white.

(IV) Winter

On the city gate a horn blows dreary and low,

Crescent moon's twilight fills half of the hall's glow,

Waterside and hillside blanketed with snow.

A bamboo-fenced cottage with wreath and wafting smoke,

It stands in the village alone.

Literary Appreciation

This collection of song poems explores the theme of the four seasons, that is, spring, summer, autumn, and winter, with simple language, clarity, and a natural flow. The first song poem portrays a picturesque scene with warm spring weather, abundant blossoms, beautiful mountains, serene waters, and energetic singing and dancing. The second shows scenes during midsummer, with people relishing a tranquil and refreshing ambiance under clear sky. The third specifically captures the desolate atmosphere of autumn, evoking a sense of lovesickness comparable to Ma Zhiyuan's *Tune: Sunny Sand Autumn Thoughts*. The fourth portrays a somber and dim winter evening landscape, with the phrase " a horn blows dreary " intensifying the melancholic atmosphere of this scene. On the whole, the author had skillfully described the landscape as it closely aligns with the distinct attributes of the four seasons while conveying emotions through the depiction of scenery, illustrating scenery through emotions, and combining dynamic and static elements. The entirety of the four song poems is predominantly described through the use of nouns, particularly when it comes to capturing scenic imagery. The absence of verbs in the song poems allows for a static and visually descriptive presentation, and the simplicity and aesthetic appeal of the language used creates a distinct and enjoyable reading experience, leaving a lasting impression on the readers.

沉醉东风

渔夫

白朴

黄芦岸白蘋渡口，

绿杨堤红蓼滩头。

虽无刎颈交，

却有忘机友，

点秋江白鹭沙鸥。

傲杀人间万户侯，

不识字烟波钓叟。

品读

　　这首曲写作者隐居江湖之乐，表现除了隐逸消沉之外的思想。作者以渔夫自比，将这一与世无争的闲逸形象置于黄芦、白蘋、绿杨、红蓼组合而成的特殊画面中，色彩鲜明，境界高雅。再以渔夫之交友，侧面表现出他的为人和品性，塑造出其高风亮节。后用轻万户侯而甘于隐身江湖作结，显得更加语气肯定，情感浓烈。通篇写景细致，意境开阔，是歌颂隐逸、寄情山水题材中的名作。

Tune: Indulged in East Wind

Fisherman

Bai Pu

Yellow reeds overgrow on the river short,

Floating grass adorns the ferry's core,

Willows shade the bank so green,

Princess—feather adorns the beach serene.

No lifelong friends have I,

My companions feel at peace with the world.

Autumn river dotted with gulls and herons white,

I look down on the lords proud of their might,

In mist and cold water, an old fisherman I be.

Literary Appreciation

Theauthor of this song poem enjoys seclusion amidst the complicated human world, as evident by the seclusion and despondency it expressed. The author draws a comparison between himself and a fisherman, and puts this carefree image in a carefully constructed image that includes elements such as yellow reeds, floating grass, green willows, and princess—feather with bright colors and delicate appearance. Then, the fisherman's friendships are described, which reveal his distinct personalities, thereby demonstrating his high moral values. Later, the speaker arrived at a conclusion, expressing his willingness to retreat to the countryside, conveying a more positive tone and intense emotions. These four song poems are meticulously depicted to showcase a broad artistic conception; they are masterpieces that explore the theme of solitude and the expression of emotions.

凭阑人

寄征衣

姚燧

欲寄君衣君不还，
不寄君衣君又寒。
寄与不寄间，
妾身千万难。

品读

　　这首小令以通俗流畅的语言、真挚自然的感情、细致入微的描写，逼真传神地刻画出一位思妇给常年在外的丈夫寄冬衣时丰富而又复杂的心理活动。通过她在"寄"与"不寄"之间的徘徊、犹豫、矛盾，表达了她对丈夫的思念和爱怜。一"欲寄"，一"不寄"；一"不还"，一"又寒"，将思妇"千万难"的这种情感描摹得淋漓尽致，惟妙惟肖。全曲仅四句，就高超地塑造出一位美丽善良而又温柔多情的闺中少妇形象，足见作者的才艺之高。卢前在《论曲绝句》中评这首曲"熨帖温存，缠绵尽致"，道出了此曲在艺术上的独到之处。

Tune: Leaning on Balustrade

The Winter Garment

Yao Sui

A winter garment for my love if I send,

He won't return when winter's chill does yearn.

If I do not, in the cold he shivers.

What shall I do?

Decisions, a challenge to take.

Literary Appreciation

This song poem vividly depicts the intricate psychological experiences of a woman who longed for her loved one, the emotions of whom expressed through the act of sending winter clothes to her husband who is constantly away. The writer employed everyday language that is eloquent to convey the woman's genuine sentiments with great detail and precision. The speaker's conflicting emotions are evident in her contemplation of whether to send or not send the winter garments, reflecting her thoughts and affection towards her husband. Similarly, the contrasting notions of worrying that her husband "won't return" or that he will "shiver" vividly depict the internal conflict experienced by a lovesick wife, encapsulating the multitude of difficulties she faces. The song poem consists of only four sentences, yet it skillfully portrays a vivid image of a beautiful, kind, empathetic, and affectionate young woman in her boudoir. This demonstrates the exceptional talent of the writer. In his work The Quatrains and Yuan Opera, Lu Qian commented on this song poem, describing it as "considerate, gentle, and with an abundance of sentimentality", while pointing out the song's artistic distinctiveness.

天净沙
秋思
马致远

枯藤老树昏鸦，

小桥流水人家，

古道西风瘦马。

夕阳西下，

断肠人在天涯。

品读

　　这首小令向来被认为是曲中杰作。作者通过简短的五句二十八个字，精彩生动地道出了一个"断肠人"在旅途上的深切感受。作品将枯藤、老树、昏鸦、小桥、流水、人家、古道、西风、瘦马、夕阳、断肠人等事物有机地联系组合在一起，既写出了时间（黄昏），又点明了季节（深秋），还说明了地点（野外），同时更刻画了人物，抒发了情感，显得精致玲珑、含蓄凝练而又丰富复杂，境界宽阔，写景与抒情达到了高度的统一与融合。此外，写景状物的出色，也在曲中表现得极为突出。作者用极省的笔墨既写黯淡悲凉的画面，又描摹闲淡安逸的场景，善于将人物置于景色之中传情表意，显得如诗如画、有声有色。在语言上颇见锤炼功夫，淡中寓雅、生动真实、传神细腻，具有丰富的艺术表现力和感染力。元人周德清在《中原音韵》中誉之为"秋思之祖"。王国维也称赞它"寥寥数语，深得唐人绝句妙境""纯是天籁，仿佛唐人绝句"，可谓知音之评。

Tune：Sunny Sand
Autumn Thoughts
Ma Zhiyuan

Over old trees with withered vines fly crows,

Under a small bridge near a cottage a stream flows,

On ancient road in the cold breeze's sway a bony horse goes.

Westwards descends the setting sun,

Far from home is a broken heart.

Literary Appreciation

This song poem has always been esteemed as a masterpiece. In five short sentences and a total of 28 words, the author concisely and vividly conveys the profound emotions experienced by a heartbroken man during his journey. It organically incorporates various elements, including withered vines, old trees, crows, bridges, flowing water, residents, roads, west winds, a bony horse, the setting sun, and a heartbroken man, through which it not only depicts the time of day (dusk), but also indicates the season (late autumn) and the setting (field). At the same time, it portrays the characters and expresses a range of emotions; it exhibits exceptional qualities, characterized by its refined, nuanced, and succinct nature, and encompasses a vast scope. The combination of scenery writing and lyricism within this song poem has achieved a remarkable level of expertise. In addition, this song poem prominently showcases exceptional scenic descriptions. The writer used highly concise language to create somber and melancholic scenes and capture serene and comfortable settings. He was proficient in positioning the characters within the scenery to convey his emotions, which is an artistic approach that results in the creation of picturesque and vivid imagery. Meanwhile, the language used in this song poem is refined, elegant, and brisk, while also displaying a wealth of artistic expression and appeal. In the *Rhymes of the Central Plains*, Zhou Deqing from the Yuan dynasty praised this song poem as the Origin of Autumn Thoughts. Wang Guowei also commended this work for its "few words that effectively captures the beauty of the quatrains of the Tang dynasty" and "heaven-made language, reminiscent of the quatrains of the Tang dynasty", which are a suited endorsement.

寿阳曲

马致远

（一）山市晴岚

花村外，

草店西，

晚霞明雨收天霁。

四围山一竿残照里，

锦屏风又添铺翠。

（二）远浦帆归

夕阳下，

酒旆闲，

两三航未曾着岸。

落花水香茅舍晚，

断桥头卖鱼人散。

（三）潇湘夜雨

渔灯暗，

客梦回，

一声声滴人心碎。

孤舟五更家万里，

是离人几行情泪。

品读

"山市晴岚"为潇湘八景之一。山市,指山中蜃景。清代周亮工《书影》卷五云:"然人知有海市,而不知有山市。东省莱潍去邑西二十里许,有孤山,上有夷齐庙。志称春夏之交,西南风微起,则孤山移影城西。从城上望之,凡山峦林木、神祠人物,无不聚现。逾数时,渐远,渐无所睹矣。"这首曲描绘了一幅山村傍晚雨过天晴后的秀美景色,如同山中的海市蜃楼一般。曲作先写山村的美丽图景,以"花""草"和"霞""雨"既点出山市的繁花似锦、碧草遍地,又写出了雨后天晴的壮观景致,交代了题目中的"晴"字。后二句则集中笔墨,重点写"晚照"装点下的山色,将落日余晖中苍翠欲滴的群山写得秀丽迷人、自然宁静、色彩鲜明。整曲虽纯用白描手法,但已使村舍茅店和晚霞青山历历在目、尽收眼底,显得生动形象、质朴明丽、清新如画,充满田园气息和美的诱惑。

"远浦帆归"为潇湘八景之一。这首小令以清淡自然的格调和明快轻松的笔法,描绘出了夕阳西下,酒旗闲挂,两三只船还在远处的海上漂泊,崖边花漂流水,卖鱼人收市回家的情景,展现出一幅宁静悠闲、格调纯朴的渔村风俗画。在写法上,作者既写出了景色,又间接点出了酒店的萧条,同时以"落花水香"极写山村的明媚可爱和美丽的自然风光,而最后一句"断桥边卖鱼人散"既点出了傍晚渔市已散的场面,又暗寓着每天出现在这里的繁华热闹和卖鱼人那高低悠扬的叫卖声。表面上写人散去,实质上正为写人;表面上写寂静无人,实质上正为表现喧闹人多。这种以无写有、以静显闹的手法,既符合整个画面的色调,又给读者提供了广阔深远的想象余地,含蓄蕴藉,生动传神。同时,作者既写远景,又描近景,显得层次清晰,色彩浓郁,具有独特的渔乡风情。

　　"潇湘夜雨"为潇湘八景之一。这首小令以低沉哀婉的基调、缠绵真切的笔触，形象地描绘出潇湘夜雨的情景，抒发客子思乡念归的感情。前三句描绘出一幅渔灯昏暗、夜雨淅沥、游子不眠的江雨图，以"渔灯"来烘托江面苍茫迷蒙的景象，以"梦回"来点染离人对家乡亲人的思念，而一"灯"一"人"都被置于淅淅沥沥、彻夜不绝的夜雨之中，更显境界朦胧而色调抑郁。尤其是"一声声""滴""碎"等字眼，更是一字千钧，将秋雨拟人化，表达出"离人"内心的痛苦，且具有声响效果和动感，使整个画面不但感情低沉，而且富有立体效果，使人如临其境、如闻其声、肝肠寸断。后二句则一写离家之远的孤独，一写相思之情的深挚，将离别之人的感情一语倾泻，表达出思念的深刻真挚。尤其是将秋雨比拟为离人之泪，更富有情韵和形象感，显得贴切自然、情景交汇。

Tune: Song of Long-lived Sun

Ma Zhiyuan

(I) Sun-Lit Mist-Veiled Mountain

In village's bloom,

West of wine's store,

Sunsets after storm, brilliant and beautiful.

Rainbow clouds after rain brighten the sky far and wide.

Surrounding hills steeped in setting sun's ray,

Embroidered screen graced by emerald green.

(II) Returning Sails

Sun sets behind the hill,

Wine store's sign, a symbol still,

Two or three fishing boats yet to come ashore.

Flowers fall, water flows, by the door,

Day's end near,

On homeward bound, fishmongers scatter.

(III) Night Rain on the River

In dim lights of the fishers' lanterns,

I wake fromdreams,

Drop by drop, raindrops fall, my heart breaks.

Deep in the night, far from home, my boat roams alone,

Tears fall like rain,

From those who are in distant lands.

Literary Appreciation

The *Sun-Lit Mist-Veiled Mountain* is one of the eight scenic spots in Hunan Province. "Mist-veiled mountain" commonly refers to a mirage occurring in mountainous regions. According to the *Book Shadow*, written by Zhou Lianggong of the Qing dynasty, "it is commonly known that a mirage can occur in the sea, yet many don't know that it can also occur in mountainous regions. Located in the eastern part of Shandong Province lies a lone mountain extending from Laiwei to a distance of 20 miles west of the city; it is home to Yiqi Temple. Between spring and summer, when the southwest wind slightly rises, the lone mountain will shift towards the west of the city. From the city, mountains, trees, and shrines could be observed throughout the area. As time progresses, the mountain moves away, eventually diminished. " This song poem depicts a picturesque setting of a mountain village during the evening after a rainfall, resembling a mirage amidst the mountains. It first describes a beautiful image of the mountain village, using the elements of flowers, grass, sunset, and rain to not only describes the abundant blooming flowers and lush green grass amidst the mountain mist, but also depicts a magnificent scene of clear weather after rainfall, thereby establishing its connection with the word "sunny" in the title. The last two sentences emphasize the picturesque view of the mountains adorned by the evening light. The verdant mountains are described as being bathed in the soft glow of the setting sun, exhibiting a captivating blend of beautiful, natural, serene, and vibrant colors. Despite being written in simple language, this song poem successfully portrays a vivid and panoramic scene featuring a thatched cottage, a sunset, and green hills, which is an imagery characterized by its simplicity, vividness, refreshness, and picturesque quality that evokes a pastoral and scenic setting.

The *Returning Sails* is one of the eight scenic spots in Hunan Province. This song poem depicts a serene fishing village scene with a simple style; it captures the setting sun, the flag of a wine store hanging idly, a few boats drifting in the distant sea, flowers swaying on the edge of a cliff, and fishmongers making their way home from the market. The writer's light and natural language, along with an animated but soft undertone, adds to the overall charm of the song poem. In terms of the writing, the writer not only depicted the idyllic scenery, but also highlighted the somber atmosphere in the wine store. At the same time, he eloquently described the picturesque natural landscape of the mountain village, as evident by the phrase "flowers fall, water flows". Furthermore, the concluding sentence, "on homeward bound, fishmongers scatter", not only describes the closure of the fishing market during the evening, but also implies the bustling daily commotion and the voices of the fishmongers in this location. At first glance, the writer wrote about scattered people, but he was essentially writing about the people's activities; he might have been describing a silence due to the lack of people, but he could have been suggesting the presence of people in a bustling market. This technique that makes something out of nothing not only aligns with the overall tone of the song poem, but also stimulates readers' imagination through vivid and expressive descriptions. The writer also skillfully presented the imagery in both macroscopic and microscopic perspective, lending the song poem its clarity, vibrant imagery, and distinctive portrayal of a fishing village ambiance.

The *Night Rain on the River* is one of the eight scenic spots in Hunan

45

Province. This song poem vividly portrays the atmospheric setting of a rainy night in Hunan, while also conveying the homesickness experienced by the travelers with a somber and poignant tone. The first three sentences paint a vivid image of restless travelers and a river shrouded in rainfall, illuminated by faint lights from fishing boats. The writer employed the lanterns on fishing boats to enhance the misty ambiance on the river's surface, and the dreams to evoke nostalgic sentiments which prompts the travelers to reminisce about their loved ones in their hometown. Furthermore, the "lantern" and the speaker are placed under the pitter-pattering night autumn rain, personified by words such as "drop by drop" "fall" and "break" which added to their subdued condition and melancholic tone, thereby effectively conveying the pain to leave from the loved ones. In addition, they create an auditory and dynamic effect, leading to a vivid and immersive depiction of the scene. As a result, the overall portrayal is not only emotionally impactful but also enables the readers to feel as though they are present in the scene, hearing the rain and experiencing the sorrow in person. Whereas the last two sentences depict the profound sense of solitude experienced when one is away from their hometown and convey the overwhelming feeling of longing for loved ones and heartache. In particular, the autumn rain is likened to tears shed during a farewell, which is a fitting and natural correlation, as the depicted scenes align and exude a captivating allure and vivid imagery.

十二月过尧民歌

别情

王实甫

（一）十二月

自别后遥山隐隐，更那堪远水粼粼。

见杨柳飞绵滚滚，对桃花醉脸醺醺。

透内阁香风阵阵，掩重门暮雨纷纷。

（二）尧民歌

怕黄昏忽地又黄昏，不销魂怎地不销魂。

新啼痕压旧啼痕，断肠人忆断肠人。

今春，香肌瘦几分，搂带宽三寸。

品读

　　这是一篇写女主人公缠绵哀怨的悲愁心情的小令。作者先以整齐的句式，描写和营造出一个由遥山、远水、杨柳、桃花环绕而成的在香风、暮雨之中的内阁、重门，以景写人，以景寓情，颇有神韵。在手法上，运用叠字，既具有鲜明的节奏美和韵律美，又增强了抒情的效果和感染力。同时在距离上，由远及近，由虚到实，颇具匠心。后段则以连续的几个重复加排比句式，直接表达女主人公内心的情感，显得抒情自然质朴而意味无穷，用字通俗生动而自出新意。曲尾以直陈式的话语作结，虽显夸张却合情入理，同时也给人无限遐想的余地。全曲音节铿锵，句式整齐，语言雅丽，措辞精彩，抒情真挚，状景生动，技法娴熟，功力纯厚。此曲在语言风格上与《西厢记》极为相似。明代朱权在《太和正音谱》中评："王实甫之词，如花间美人。铺叙委婉，深得骚人之趣。极有佳句，若玉环之出浴华清，绿珠之采莲洛浦。"周德清《中原音韵》评此曲"对偶、音律、平仄、语句皆妙"。

From A Year's End to Folklore

Parting Grief

Wang Shifu

(I) Tune: A Years's End

Since we parted, mountains loom in the distance beyond my reach.

How can I bear the stream's rippling view?

Willow catkins waft on waves,

Flushed cheeks, drunk on peach blossom's grace,

Fragrant breeze journeys my boudoir, now and then,

Evening rain falls on my closed door, once and again.

(II) Tune: Folklore

The dusk's swift arrival I fear,

To spare my soul from woe I hope.

Days spent in tears, a constant flow of sorrow,

One broken heart yearns for kindred's soul.

This spring,

My body tale's unfolds,

My girdle once snug, now three inches wider they hold.

Literary Appreciation

This song poem delves into the melancholic emotional state of the speaker. First, the writer presented a vivid depiction of a boudoir and its heavy doors, situated amidst a landscape of distant mountains, waters, willows, and peach blossoms with fragrant breezes and dusk rain, through meticulous use of sentence structures. His depiction of people through their surroundings, as well as ability to evoke emotions through the scenes, exudes a captivating allure. As for writing technique, the use of reduplicative words not only lends the song poem a distinctive aesthetic quality in terms of rhythm and cadence, but also enhances its lyrical impact and appeal. The writer also took an ingenious artistic approach to present scenes from far to near and from virtual to real. In the latter part of the song poem, the speaker's internal emotions are conveyed in simple everyday language through repetition and parallel sentences, which adds a lyrical quality to the song poem while exhibiting naturalness, simplicity, and depth. The song poem concludes with direct and exaggerated yet well-judged words, providing ample room for imaginative interpretation. Overall, the song poem was written with sonorous syllables, well-structured sentence patterns, refined language, captivating wording, heartfelt lyricism, vivid imagery, adept techniques, and impeccable skills. The linguistic style of this song poem bears a striking resemblance to that of the *Romance of the Western Chamber*. During the Ming dynasty, Zhu Quan commented in his work *A Formulary for the Correct Sounds of Great Harmony* that "the linguistic expression used in Wang Shifu's poem is comparable to a beautiful woman amidst an array of flowers". His use of euphemism has garnered the attention and interest of writers. His sentences are of such excellent proficiency that they are often likened to the exquisite beauty of Yuhuan bathing in the Huaqing Pool and the elegance of Lyuzhu gathering lotus flowers along Luopu. In Zhou Deqing's *Rhymes of the Central Plains*, it is stated that this particular song poem exhibits "exceptional qualities in terms of antithesis, temperament, prosody, and sentence structure".

寿阳曲

答卢疏斋

珠帘秀

山无数，

　烟万缕，

　憔悴煞玉堂人物。

　倚篷窗一身儿活受苦，

　恨不得随大江东去。

品读

　　这首小令是珠帘秀为答卢挚《寿阳曲·别珠帘秀》一曲而写的。曲作以寓情于景的写法，通过对送别者和离别者之间细腻感情心理的形象刻画，表达了知音般的难舍难分之情。曲的开头二句，以触目之景写离别之情，情景交融，渲染气氛。中间一句承卢挚曲意，写他当时的心理痛苦。"憔悴"一词，括尽别后情状，抵上千言万语。结尾二句则从双方来写，既写被送别者依依不舍的苦痛酸楚，又写送别者不忍分离、痛不欲生的情感。全曲感情真切诚挚，自然直率，描景凝练，写人生动，语言朴素浅显，形象鲜明，尤其是描摹双方的心理，更显作者的艺术才华和深厚功力。

Tune: Song of Long-lived Sun

A Reply to Lu Zhi

Zhu Lianxiu

Manifold mountains,

And wreaths of smoke,

Your gaunt appearance, I cannot see.

Heart broken, I leaned on the casement's ledge.

In river's embrace I seek release, with waves that journey east.

Literary Appreciation

Written by Zhu Lianxiu as a response to Lu Zhi's *Farewell to Zhu Lianxiu*, this song poem expresses the emotions experienced by the writer through vivid descriptions of the scene, and delves into the intricate emotions and psychological dynamics between the sender off and the leaver, effectively conveying a sense of close companionship. The first two sentences effectively convey the sentiment of separation through a poignant portrayal; the scenes and emotions perfectly merge to create a compelling ambiance. The next sentence is the writer's direct response to Lu Zhi's song poem, which described his distress at the time. Her choice of "gaunt appearance" is highly evocative, encapsulating a multitude of situations that have happened after their separation. The final two sentences reflect the emotions experienced by both sides, encompassing not only the pain and sorrow felt by the one bidding farewell, but also the anguish experienced by those who find it difficult to bear the im-

53

pending separation. This song poem exudes sincerity and genuine emotions through a natural and straightforward approach, with concise and vivid descriptions of scenery, despite the simple language employed. In particular, the song poem effectively captures the emotions of both sides involved, thereby showcasing the writer's artistic talent and profound expertise.

得胜令

四月一日喜雨

张养浩

万象欲焦枯，

一雨足沾濡。

天地回生意，

风云起壮图。

农夫，舞破蓑衣绿；

和余，欢喜的无是处。

品读

这是一首悯农曲。全曲以通俗浅近、明白如话的语言，描摹出作者与农民一起在大旱之时喜逢甘霖的欢快高兴的场景，表现出作者对老百姓疾苦的关注和同情。曲的开头二句，先言世间万物在烈日的炙烤下，都已近焦枯，次言一场好雨滋润大地，将作者的急切和欢畅心情，逼真写出。接下二句续写在雨露的湿润下，大地又充满了勃勃生机，人们对未来满怀希望。结尾四句，以热烈的笔触，既描写农民们得雨后的狂喜欢腾之景，又展现出作者无以复加的欢欣喜悦之情，怜农悯农之心，跃然纸上。据史载，此曲写于作者晚年关中大旱入陕赈灾之际。同时张养浩还写有散套《南吕·一枝花·咏喜雨》，也表现了他对民生疾苦的关心，可以参照。

Tune: Song of Triumph

Auspicious Rain on First Day of Fourth Month

Zhang Yanghao

All plants wither and dry,

Rain falls, earth's thirst quenched.

World brims with life' vigor,

Wind and cloud bring mirth.

Farmers danced in tattered coir raincoats,

In blissful trance, I find delight,

Joy filled their hearts, my own accord.

Literary Appreciation

This songpoem is an expression of empathy for farmers. In everyday language, it depicts a joyful setting in which the writer and the farmers enjoy the rain amidst a period of drought, effectively conveying the writer's genuine concern and empathy towards the hardships faced by the common people. The first two sentences first depict a world almost parched due to the scorching sun, then state that rainfall has provided much-needed moisture to the earth, through which the writer's eagerness and joy are vividly portrayed. The next two sentences described the wet rain and dew, after which the earth is brimmed with vitality, and people are full of hope for the future. The last four sentences artistically depict the elation experienced by the farmers following the rainfall, and convey the writer's overwhelming joy and compassion for the farmers. Historical records documented that this song poem was written in the writer's later years, when he traveled to Shaanxi to alleviate the severe drought in the Guanzhong region. He also wrote another song poem entitled A Sprig of Flower: Praise Auspicious Rain, which, too, reflects his concern for people's livelihood.

山坡羊
潼关怀古
张养浩

峰峦如聚，

波涛如怒，

山河表里潼关路。

望西都，

意踟蹰。

伤心秦汉经行处，

宫阙万间都做了土。

兴，

百姓苦；

亡，

百姓苦。

品读

　　这首小令作于作者赴陕赈灾途中，是一首怀古抒情的名篇。作者先以眼中所见起头，写潼关的险要形势。第一句写山，将众多山峰攒聚一起、层峦叠嶂的景象写得生动传神，气势不凡。尤其着一"聚"字，既有动感，又凝重庄严，寓静于动，恰切准确。第二句写水，重点突出黄河的水流湍急、汹涌奔腾，一个"怒"字，既有音响效果，又侧面烘托出作者心潮澎湃、悲愤填膺的吊古伤今之情。第三句山水合写，嵌典故于行文之中，自然流畅、不露痕迹。以下两句抒写作者情怀，作者望着古都长安，思绪万千，心情沉重。"伤心"两句，正面表达出作者"意踌躇"的内容：面对秦汉以来连年征战的这块土地，联想到多少王朝兴衰隆替，但如今都成为焦土遗迹，不禁伤感痛心。最后以无论"兴""亡"百姓都受灾难的深痛慨叹，表现出对历史的深刻反思和锐利洞察。这一结尾，含义丰富，情感愤激，精辟透彻，耐人寻味。全曲既是对历史的追忆和评价，也是对当时现实社会状况的无情揭露，风格刚健，语言质朴，抒情自然，堪为力作。

Tune: Sheep on Mountain Slope
Meditation on the Past at Tong Pass
Zhang Yanghao

Massed peaks and ridges,

Raging waves and torrents,

Between the mountains and the rivers,

On the road through Tong Pass I appear.

I look to the western Capital,

My thoughts unsettled.

In ancient lands of Qin and Han,

Palaces and terraces now mere dust.

Empire rises,

People's plight;

Empire falls,

Suffering's height.

Literary Appreciation

This song poem written by the writer during his journey to Shaanxi Province for providing disaster relief is renowned for its meditation and lyrical poetry. He began by providing an account of what he saw, then delved into a depiction of the dangerous situations in the Tong Pass. The first sentence describes the mountains, depicting a vivid image of many peaks and ridges congregating together, exhibiting remarkable energy and might. The term

"massed" used in this sentence is appropriate in that it is dynamic and impos-
ing, portraying a tranquil scene through an impactful image. The second sentence focuses on the quick and turbulent nature of the Yellow River's flow.
The term "raging" used in this sentence not only creates an immersive setting
for the readers, but also emphasizes the emotional intensity experienced by the
writer, including his distress and righteous indignation. The third sentence
seamlessly combines references to mountains and rivers, incorporating
allusions in a natural and fluid manner. The next two sentences express the
writer's sentiments. He turned to look towards Chang'an, the historical capital
of multiple dynasties, prompting a multitude of thoughts that weighed heavily
on their mind. The sentence "in ancient lands of Qin and Han" effectively
conveys the essence of the writer's "unsettled thoughts". In other words,
when thinking of the enduring conflict that has plagued this land since the Qin
and Han dynasties, one cannot help but reflect upon the cyclical nature of the
rise and fall of the numerous dynasties, and acknowledge that the once pros-
perous land had turned into a wasteland, evoking a sense of sorrow in the writer. Finally, the song poem concludes with a lamentation regarding the plight
of the common people, emphasizing that they endure the most suffering regardless of whether an empire "rises" or "falls", which demonstrates the writer's
thoughtful reflection and keen understanding of historical events. The conclusion of this song poem exhibits a profound depth of significance, evoking
strong emotions and inciting deep contemplation. This song poem is both a
meditation and assessment of historical events, as well as a ruthless revelation
of the prevailing societal conditions during that period. It is a masterpiece
characterized by its dynamic style, simple language, and natural lyricism.

鹦鹉曲

白贲

侬家鹦鹉洲边住，

是个不识字渔父。

浪花中一叶扁舟，

睡煞江南烟雨。

觉来时满眼青山，

抖擞绿蓑归去。

算从前错怨天公，

甚也有安排我处。

品读

这是一首很有名的小令，唱和者众，冯子振曾和四十二首之多。曲作情景相融，感情坦率，语言通俗，寄托遥深。开头二句以自述口吻，点明人物、地点，虽平淡如话，却包含着对世事的不平之情。中间四句直叙渔父闲适自由的生活，写得颇具诗情画意，很有恬静的田园之趣。结尾二语以自嘲口气，充满慰藉和调侃之意，但同时也外露着抑郁愤懑之情，表面上旷达，其实充满着对现实的关注。朱权《太和正音谱》谓其词"孑然独立，峣然挺出，若孤峰之插晴昊，使人莫不仰视也"。观此曲，也可体味其独特、不凡的创作风格。

Tune: Song of Parrot

Bai Ben

In Parrot Island I reside,

An illiterate fisherman I stride.

My boat, brave perilous waves,

Southern rain's mist, in sleep I embrace,

When awake, eyes filled with cleared sky's grace,

I return, shedding rain from my coat of coir.

In days of old, I blamed Heaven's name,

But my error, I now proclaim,

As His will a masterful display.

Literary Appreciation

The tune this song poem was set on holds significant renown and had been written by many writers, including Feng Zizhen who had written as much as 42 other song poems in this tune. The lyrics and scenes within the song poem are seamlessly integrated, the emotions portrayed are sincere and genuine, the language is relatable to common people, and the depth of the content is thought-provoking. It begins with a narration which points out the people and places involved, and expresses an indignation towards worldly matters, despite the simplicity of the language. The next four sentences describe the speaker's leisurely and free life, evoking a sense of poetry and idyllic tranquility. Mean-

63

while, the final two sentences exhibit a self-deprecating tone that combines elements of consolation and mockery, while revealing deeper emotions of depression and resentment. At first glance, the writer appears to be open and accepting, but it is evident that he is deeply concerned for the reality. Zhu Quan's *A Formulary for the Correct Sounds of Great Harmony* pointed out that the words used in this song poem are "distinctive and prominent" and "comparable to isolated peaks placed in a sunny location, where people will naturally look up towards it". This song poem is distinctive and exceptional in its artistic approach.

鹦鹉曲

山亭逸兴

冯子振

嵯峨峰顶移家住，

是个不唧溜樵父。

烂柯时树老无花，

叶叶枝枝风雨。

故人曾唤我归来，

却道不如休去。

指门前万叠云山，

是不费青蚨买处。

品读

　　这套小令是和白贲的《鹦鹉曲》的。曲前有小序，可见白词之佳，但冯词续得也不差，且一连四十余首，充分显示了作者不凡的文思才华。这是第一首，全篇运用烂柯樵夫的典故，表现出了与世隔绝的隐士闲淡祥和的生活。开头二句塑造樵夫形象，质朴豁达，远离尘世。接着二句刻画老树形象，写其历经人间风雨寒霜，饱受苦难磨炼，借景抒情，以树拟人，词人感慨，发诸笔端。后两句直抒对现实社会的不满和愤懑，表达自己向往青山绿水的宁静闲适生活的态度。结尾二句，以不用金钱就可拥有"万叠云山"，进一步表明了作者甘愿隐居、不慕权贵和金钱的思想。全曲风格豪放洒脱，节奏明快，写景抒情，自然畅达，语言通俗生动而又雅丽含蓄，读之顿觉超逸雄放、豪情满怀。

Tune: Song of Parrot

A Recluse's Delight in the Mountain Pavilion

Feng Zizhen

My house, atop the frowning hill,

A woodman, I lack the skill.

I play chess as flowers fall from old trees,

Branch by branch, leaf by leaf, in rain and breeze.

Friends beckoned me back,

but I would rather stay.

Chain of mountains and clouds, a sight to behold before my door,

Without spending a single coin, a wonderful sight I adore.

Literary Appreciation

This song poem is the first of a series of continuation of Bai Ben's *Song of Parrot*. It is preceded by a preface, which highlights the exceptional quality of Bai's lyrics. However, Feng's continuation is also worthy of praise; this continuation includes over 40 song poems, which showcased his remarkable literary talent. This song poem employs allusions to the woodman, illustrating the serene and tranquil life of a recluse who secluded from the outside world. The first two sentences portray the woodcutter as a person with a straightforward and open demeanor, distanced from the complexities of the world, while the next two sentence portrays an image of an old tree, highlighting its endurance through hardships in the world, effectively conveying the writer's emotions by leveraging the surrounding landscape and personifying trees as people. The following two sentences directly express discontent and resentment towards the actual society, while indicating a longing for a tranquil and leisure life amidst verdant mountains and flowing waters. Meanwhile, the writer stated in the last two sentence that one can own a "chain of mountains" without worldly means, which reinforce his willingness towards seclusion and a lack of appreciation for wealth and influence. This song poem is characterized by a bold and free style, lively rhythm, and lyrical scenery, and is written in natural and eloquent everyday language, while also managing to be vivid and nuanced, evoking a transcendent experience imbued with a sense of pride and bravery in the readers.

哨遍
高祖还乡
睢景臣

（一）

社长排门告示，

但有的差使无推故。

这差使不寻俗：

一壁厢纳草除根，

一边又要差夫，

索应付。

又言是车驾，

都说是銮舆，

今日还乡故。

王乡老执定瓦台盘，

赵忙郎抱着酒葫芦。

新刷来的头巾，

恰糨来的绸衫，

畅好是妆幺大户。

（二）耍孩儿

瞎王留引定火乔男女，

胡踢蹬吹笛擂鼓。

见一彪人马到庄门，

匹头里几面旗舒。

一面旗白胡阑

套住个迎霜兔，

一面旗红曲连

打着个毕月乌。

一面旗鸡学舞，

一面旗狗生双翅，

一面旗蛇缠葫芦。

（三）五煞

红漆了叉，

银铮了斧，

甜瓜苦瓜黄金镀。

明晃晃马镫枪尖上挑，

白雪雪鹅毛扇上铺。

这几个乔人物，

拿着些不曾见的器仗，

穿着些大作怪衣服。

（四）四煞

辕条上都是马，

套顶上不见驴，

黄罗伞柄天生曲。

车前八个天曹判，

车后若干递送夫。

更几个多娇女，

一般穿着，

一样妆梳。

（五）三煞

那大汉下的车，

众人施礼数。

那大汉觑得人如无物。

众乡老展脚舒腰拜，

那大汉挪身着手扶。

猛可里抬头觑，

觑多时认得，

险气破我胸脯。

（六）二煞

你身须姓刘，

你妻须姓吕。

把你两家儿根脚从头数。

你本身做亭长耽几盏酒，

你丈人教村学读几卷书。

曾在俺庄东住，

也曾与我喂牛切草，

拽坝扶锄。

（七）一煞

春采了桑，

冬借了俺粟。

零支了米麦无重数。

换田契强称了麻三秤，

还酒债偷量了豆几斛。

有甚胡突处？

明标着册历，

现放着文书。

（八）尾声

少我的钱差发内旋拨还，

欠我的粟税粮中私准除。

只道刘三，

谁肯把你揪捽住？

白甚么改了姓更了名，

唤做汉高祖！

品读

这是一首极为著名的套曲。曲作以纯朴憨厚的庄稼人口吻，通过他们的所见所想，以泼辣大胆的语言和白描细腻的刻画，塑造出了一代统治者刘邦的形象，揭穿了这位天朝皇帝的无赖底细，文笔滑稽幽默，思想犀利深刻。作者先以夸大之笔极写这位大人物给乡民带来的繁忙和紧张，以社长、王乡老、赵忙郎等人的慎重表现，烘托出一种神秘庄严的气氛，可谓以虚写实、欲抑先扬。而后以乡民陌生的眼光和轻视的口吻，描写皇家的乐队和旗队、仪仗队、车前驾后的侍卫官女，层次清楚，笔调活泼多趣，俗中带讥，语中含贬。写刘邦的傲慢和无礼，但作者并不直呼其名，而是先极写其接受乡民跪拜的高傲态度，接着以"抬头觑""觑多时"两个动作，用"险气破我胸脯"一句道破，使全曲情感走向顶峰，同时也点出了这些"乔人物"簇拥下的所谓主人公，蓄势而发，极尽奇巧。接下来的两支曲一写刘邦的出身，一写他的无赖行为。作者以嘲弄、揭底的方式，将这位神秘人物置于光天化日之下，笔调辛辣，语气坚决。最后一曲通过讨债的方式，表现出作者对刘邦的不敬和鄙夷。全曲诙谐泼辣，本色当行，描写精彩生动，叙事简练，抒情自然，颇有特色。《录鬼簿》言"维扬诸公，俱作《高祖还乡》套数，惟公《哨遍》制作新奇，诸公皆出其下"。

Tune: Whistling Around

Tune: Emperor Gaozu Returns Home

Sui Jingchen

(I)

Door to door the village chief announces,

Whatever errand no one should refuse to run.

The errand is never like what we had before:

Leaf fodder be collected on the one hand;

On the other messengers should meet the demand.

Hard to deal with! They say.

The royal cortege will come,

With the emperor to his home today.

Villager Wang's hands cradle an earthen tray,

Villager Zhao, a gourd of wine.

Hood recently washed,

Silk shirt stiffened and fine,

All play the rich, despite poor in gold.

(II) Tune: Playing the Child

Youngsters lead, in strange array,

Messing around, drum beat and flute played.

A troop of horsemen arrived at the gate then,

And at their head Many banners outspread:

73

On the moon flag a jade hare in a ring white,

On the sun flag a golden crow in crimson light,

On the phoenix flag a cock dances and sings,

On the tiger flag there's a dog with two wings,

On the dragon flag you will find,

A snake around a gourd wind.

(Ⅲ) Tune: Last Stanza But Five

Fork painted red,

Ax silver—white,

Hammer like golden melon,

With stirrup bright in a guard of honour.

Plume fans, white as snow,

Flag—bearers, in motley dress,

With unseen staffs, they progress.

(IV) Tune: Last Stanza But Four

In the crossbar of shafts all steeds,

In harness there's no donkey,

Above crooked pole, yellow canopy.

Before the carriage, eight guards lead,

Behind follow attendants in livery.

And charming maids and lasses,

In matching dress and tresses.

(V) Tune: Last Stanza But Three

From the carriage a burly man comes down,

Greeted with homage by people from the town.

Blind to those who kowtow, the man fails to know.

Legs apart, villagers bow,

To help them up, forward he goes.

In an instant, I gaze above,

I gaze at him, so long,

My heart swells with anger strong.

(VI) Tune: Last Stanza But Two

Your surname Liu,

Your wife's Lyu.

I know your family's root, you see.

Fond of wine, you ruled three miles around,

Young minds' key to knowledge's door, your father-in-law.

East of my farm, you dwelled,

Cattles you fed and fodder you cut for the cow,

And lands you tilled with plow.

(VII) Tune: Last Stanza But One

In spring you picked mulberry leaf,

In winter you borrowed millet from me.

On credit you bought rice and wheat.

Renewing land deed, you took thirty-three pounds of ramie through deceit,

To pay your debt, you stole more beans and peas.

Why play the fool, I ask of thee?

In the account book, it's duly listed,

If doubt resides within, cast your gaze upon this scene.

(VIII) Tune: Epilogue

Money you owe, pay me immediately,

Taxes on my millet and pea, lower promptly.

Third born in the Liu family,

Holding you tight, I won't release you on your word.

Why change your name,

And steal an emperor's fame?

Literary Appreciation

This is asong poem famous for its portrayal of Liu Bang, the ruler of his time, through the perspective of humble and sincere peasants. The writer skillfully employed provocative and bold language with intricate descriptions to depict Liu and adeptly exposed the deceitful nature of the emperor through a combination of humorous writing and insightful thoughts. He first exaggerated the hectic schedule and heightened anxiety that this prominent figure brought to the village, creating an unsettling and solemn setting through the careful execution of the village chief, villagers Wang and Zhao, and other characters. This technique can be characterized as a form of virtual realism, aiming to both suppress and promote certain elements. Then, through a peasant's eyes and disdainful tone, the narrative proceeds to delineate the presence of the royal band and flag team, the honor guard, as well as the bodyguards and servants both in front of and behind the carriage. It has distinctive structure and lively and engaging tone, yet vulgar, contemptuous, and derogatory language. The writer discussed Liu's arrogance and rudeness, although he did not explicitly refer to Liu's name. Instead, he first wrote about Liu's haughty demeanor in readily accepting the villagers' kowtow, and elevated the song poem's sentiments by the two phrases, "I gaze above" and "so long" as well as "my heart swells with anger strong". He also highlighted the so-called great one, encircled by "flag-bearers" who were prepared to put on an act. The next two song poems delve into Liu's background and his misconducts; the writer presents this enigmatic character in a satirical approach through a witty but resolute tone. Whereas the last song poem reveals the writer's disrespect and disdain towards Liu through debt collection. Overall, these song poems are witty and vitriolic, with its unique character, showcasing remarkable and vivid descriptions, along with a concise and natural narrative. According to the Register of Spectrum, "the lords of Weiyang have written sets of Emperor Gaozu Returns Home, but Sui's novel approach in Whistling Around stands out from the rest."

殿前欢

刘时中

醉颜酡，

太翁庄上走如梭。

门前几个官人坐，

有虎皮驮驮。

呼王留唤伴哥，

无一个，空叫得喉咙破。

人踏了瓜果，马践了田禾。

品读

　　这首小令揭露了元朝社会黑暗的一个侧面，即官吏劫掠乡里、骚扰百姓的现象，描写生动，语言通俗，活灵活现，具有较高的社会认知价值和批判意义。历代官吏扰民的事件多有发生，但在元代，这种情形尤为突出，因为元代统治者系游牧地区入主中原，他们中的一些人征服、侵略积习难改，加之法定的民族压迫、民族歧视，地方百姓受欺压、受勒索是时时发生的事。刘时中曲中记录下的只是小小一桩，但也能让读者管中窥豹，略见一斑。从曲中提到的"虎皮驮驮"看，这伙人必是特权人物。他们来到一个村庄，喝得醉醺醺的，横冲直撞，掠来的东西装满了虎皮包裹，还坐在门前摆威风，到处找人。但村民们一个个早都躲开了，找不着人，于是便拿庄稼撒气，"人踏了瓜果，马践了田禾"。对此，受害的百姓能怎么样呢？写散曲的刘时中又能怎么样呢？

Tune: Joy before Palace

Liu Shizhong

Drunk red faces,

Tax collectors roam in the village.

Officials gather in the hall,

Bags of tiger skin rest, heavy and tall.

Roll called, they shout and yell,

Until their throats parched,

None answer and silent echoes.

So crop damaged, trod by horses.

Field barren, nothing could grow.

Literary Appreciation

This song poem reveals a somber aspect of the Yuan dynasty society, specifically the occurrence of officials looting villages and harassing the people, through vivid description using everyday language, thereby enabling it to hold considerable social cognitive value and carry critical significance. Throughout history, there have been many instances of officials causing disturbances among the people. However, this issue was particularly pronounced during the Yuan dynasty, which can be attributed to the fact that the rulers of the Yuan dynasty originated from nomadic regions and subsequently occupied the Central Plains. They invade and conquer, and their inherently aggressive tendencies proved difficult to alter. Furthermore, as a result of the prevailing legal framework promoting ethnic oppression and discrimination, the local community suffered from persistent oppression and coercion. What recorded in this song poem is only a minor incident, yet it effectively portrays the full picture to the readers. Judging from the "bags of tiger skin" mentioned in the song poem, these people must have been privileged. They were drunk and rampaged when they arrived at the village, and they robbed the locals to fill their tiger skin bags, even sitting in front of the doors and looking for potential victims. Nevertheless, the villagers had managed to hide themselves, so the louts were unable to find any victims. Consequently, they vented their frustration on crops, specifically "crop damaged, trod by horses. Field barren, nothing could grow". Regrettably, despite being recorded in this song poem, there was nothing the victims, or even the writer, could do about these occurrences.

醉太平
寒食
王元鼎

声声啼乳鸦，
生叫破韶华。
夜深微雨润堤沙，
香风万家。
画楼洗尽鸳鸯瓦，
彩绳半湿秋千架。
觉来红日上窗纱，
听街头卖杏花。

品读

寒食，在清明前一日（一说为前二日），正是一年春好处，春雨润物无声，春风吹香盈门，花正红，日正丽，空气正清新，景物正明净，处处怡人；再往后，春事渐歇，难免绿肥红瘦。王元鼎此曲，写寒食日的清晨，自己被一阵乳鸦声从酣梦中唤醒，想起昨宵的微雨，嗅到醉人的花香，瞥见屋顶洁净的鸳鸯瓦，庭间彩绳半湿的秋千架，发觉红日已映上自己的窗纱，正错愕间，忽然听见街头传来叫卖杏花的吆喝，顿然觉出春色的无限美好，而又暗惜其短促易逝。全曲意境从陆游诗"小楼一夜听春雨，深巷明朝卖杏花"引申而出，而画面更添富丽。

Tune: Drunk in Time of Peace

Cold Food Festival

Wang Yuanding

Nursling crows caw,

Breaking the springday's dawn.

Last night, drizzle kissed sand far and nigh,

Breeze on wings sweetened homes.

Paired tiles of painted house washed clean,

Colored ropes of swing wet before the bower.

On the window screen, I wake to see the sun's crimson glow,

In the street, cries to sell apricot flowers echo.

Literary Appreciation

Cold Food Festival, which occurs on the day preceding (or two days before) Qingming Festival, is a notable highlight of the spring season, during which the gentle rain moistens the surroundings, accompanied by a refreshing breeze that carries a delightful fragrance; the blossoms gracefully unfold, basking in the warm rays of the sun; the air is fresh, and the landscape reveals a vibrant and pristine beauty, creating an overall pleasantness. Later, when summer draws near, the scenery will not be as aesthetically pleasing as before. This song poem centers around a particular morning wherein the writer awakened from a deep slumber due to the cawing crows. He then recalled the light rainfall during the previous night, smelled the flower fragrance, caught a glimpse of the paired tiles that had been cleaned and the swing frames adorned with slightly damped colorful ropes, and noticed that the sun had cast its reflection onto the window screens. While taken aback, he heard the cries of the vendors selling apricot flowers on the street. In that moment, the writer realized the profound beauty of the spring scenery, although soon he regretted it as he also understood how brief and fleeting this beauty would be. The artistic conception of this song poem was derived from and built upon Lu You's "spring rain whispers, in a small building I listened all night, apricot flowers sold, in a deep alley when morning arrives".

塞鸿秋

薛昂夫

功名万里忙如燕，
斯文一脉微如线。
光阴寸隙流如电，
风雪两鬓白如练。
尽道便休官，
林下何曾见？
至今寂寞彭泽县。

品读

此曲意在讽刺那些热衷功名而高言归隐的人。

归隐，是元曲中最常见的主题，便是薛昂夫自己也写过不少赞美隐逸生活的散曲，但口里唱着归隐的清高调子的人，未必都心口如一，许多人吃不着葡萄便说葡萄酸地蔑视功名，有的人更是以退为进，以归隐的言辞邀功邀名。薛昂夫此曲快人快语，一下子揭穿了那些假高士的把戏，读来分外痛快淋漓。《塞鸿秋》曲牌，七句六韵，且皆为去声，繁密短促，流畅而小有顿挫，正好与曲词内在的情绪一致。

Tune: Autumn Swan on Frontier

Xue Angfu

Busy as the swallows soar, high-ranking officials, forevermore,

Culture's grace, ignored by all.

Swift as light, time takes flight,

Like frosted silk, hair turns white.

Retirement, a notion praised by all,

Yet reclusion, a path few choose to stroll.

Up to now only

The hermit of out- of- this- world still feels lonely.

Literary Appreciation

This song poem critiques those who are keen on fame and power despite frequently expressing their intentions to retire.

The theme of seclusion is prevalent in *yuanqu*, particularly in the works of Xue Angfu. He had written a number of *sanqu* that praises reclusive life. However, people who espouse the notion of seclusion may not always be as honest as their professed intentions; many despise fame and power and openly express their preference for seclusion because of resentment or disappointment stemming from their inability to attain such positions. This song poem is a captivating and delightful piece that exposes the tricks of the deceptive scholar -officials. It is set in the tune of *Autumn Swan on Frontier*, with a total of seven sentences, six rhymes, and four tones, which contributes to its compact and concise sentence structure, and smooth yet slightly tinged with frustration melody, perfectly aligning with the emotional depth conveyed by the lyrics.

沉醉东风

秋日湘阴道中

赵善庆

山对面蓝堆翠岫，

草齐腰绿染沙洲。

傲霜橘柚青，

濯雨兼葭秀。

隔沧波隐隐江楼。

点破潇湘万顷秋，

是几叶儿传黄败柳。

品读

此曲描摹潇湘初秋景色，色调浓郁，画面生动，于"万类霜天竞自由"的勃勃生机中，略略透露出一点凋残的消息，不同于习见的悲秋之作，独具一种积极的美感价值。"山对面蓝堆翠岫"，起首一句，句法奇崛，意象鲜明，很显作者不凡身手。"山对面"的"对"，当读如动词，这样"蓝堆翠岫"的山色，就仿佛是扑面迎来，正是人行山道中的动态感受。翠岫是一个描写山色的寻常词语，但在前面加上一个"蓝堆"，则增添出了无限的表现力，"堆"字既有动感，又有体积感，用在这里，让人感觉那层层山峰林嶂有一种活动的生命气息。"蓝"字则让人联想到白居易"春来江水绿如蓝"的那种明丽色泽，也让人想到远山深谷上空那一层淡淡的烟霭。

Tune: Indulged in East Wind

An Autumn Day on My Way to Xiangyin
Zhao Shanqing

Green hills rise, piled upon blue mound,

Isles with waist-deep grass, nearby found.

Tangerines and shaddocks, frost-kissed and bright,

Reeds, refreshed by rain, glisten in the light.

Across the waves, clouds dim the riverside tower.

Autumn is coming to Dongting Lake,

Withered willow leaves, a few to see.

Literary Appreciation

This song poem portrays the picturesque autumn landscape of Dongting Lake and its surrounding regions with vibrant colors and vivid imagery. In this vibrant and energetic concept of "everything living freely under freezing skies", there is a subtle indication of decline, which is artistically different from the melancholic undertones commonly seen in works associated with the autumn season. The first sentence of this song poem has an unusual syntax and presents vivid imagery, showcasing the writer's exceptional talent. The term "piled" in the sentence should be interpreted as a verb, which will create an immersive scene of the mountainous landscape of "green hills piled upon blue mound", thereby reconstructing the scenery experienced by the writer. The term "green hills" is commonly used to describe mountains. However, when used in combination with "blue mound", its impact is significantly enhanced. Meanwhile, the term "pile" conveys both dynamic sentiments and magnitude perception. When employed in this context, it evokes a sense of vibrant vitality within the summits. The term "blue" not only reminds people of Bai Juyi's vivid descriptions of "the river is so green it appears to be blue during spring", but it also brings to mind the subtle mist that often envelops the far－off mountains and valleys.

人月圆

春晚次韵

张可久

萋萋芳草春云乱，

愁在夕阳中。

短亭别酒，

平湖画舫，

垂柳骄骢。

一声啼鸟，

一番夜雨，

一阵东风。

桃花吹尽，

佳人何在，

门掩残红。

品读

　　这是一首怀人之作，一种淡淡的忧伤混融着回味的甘美，弥散在春晚的夕阳芳草中，缠绵悱恻，楚楚动人。"萋萋芳草春云乱，愁在夕阳中"，是睹景生情的起兴句，但自然景物的描绘中也渗透着浓厚的文化韵味。"萋萋芳草"，不免使人联想起《楚辞·招隐士》的"王孙游兮不归，春草生兮萋萋"和王维《送别》的"春草明年绿，王孙归不归"。春草萋萋，春云乱飞，但怀念中的那人却还杳无音信，夕阳西下，使人更添愁绪。"短亭别酒，平湖画舫，垂柳骄骢"是回思当日送别时的情景，一切恍若还在目前，但离人仍是远去不归，只留下寂寞和惆怅陪伴着自己。"一声啼鸟，一番夜雨，一阵东风"正是那一份寂寞、感伤情怀的表现。"桃花吹尽，佳人何在，门掩残红"，化用了崔护故事，使那一种寂寞怅惘的心绪显得更加具体。

Tune: Man and Moon

Rhyming with A Friend in Late Spring

Zhang Kejiu

The fragrant grass is in chaos in spring clouds,

Grief seems exhaled in the setting sun.

In the pavilion where we drank farewell,

I see the original boat in Pinghu,

Nor the proud steed neighing beneath willow trees.

I only hear the cry of birds suddenly,

The dripping rain leftover last night,

And the sigh of the eastern breeze.

All the peach flowers are blown out.

Where is the beauty of the bygone day?

Within the closed door only the fallen reds stay.

Literary Appreciation

This song poem evokes a sentimental atmosphere, characterized by a gentle melancholy and a lingering, touching aftereffect. The first two sentences, "the fragrant grass is in chaos in spring clouds, grief seems exhaled in the setting sun", as introductory sentences, express emotions evoked by the spring landscape, a depiction which also carries a strong cultural charm. The phrase "the fragrant grass is in chaos" inevitably brings to mind the line "Prince of Friends are still in traveling, the grass grows in chaos during spring" from

Chuci's "Summons for a Recluse" and "grasses return green again in the next spring, but my Prince of Friends, do you come back or not?" by Wang Wei. The grasses are blooming, and the clouds are moving swiftly across the sky, but the speaker still have not heard from their traveling loved one. This emotion of sadness is further intensified by the setting sun. The scene of bidding farewell is re – accounted through "farewell to wine in a small pavilion, original boat in Pinghu, the proud steed, neighing beneath willow trees", and everything appeared to be frozen at the time. However, the speaker is still separated with their loved one, and is accompanied solely by feelings of loneliness and melancholy. The sentences "the cry of birds suddenly, the dripping rain leftover last night and the sigh of the eastern breeze" serves as an expression of this lonesome and sentimental emotion. Whereas the sentences "Where is the beauty of the bygone day? Within the closed door only the fallen reds stay" are inspired by Cui Hu's poem, a narrative used to enhance the depiction of a desolate and melancholic ambiance.

普天乐
西湖即事
张可久

蕊珠宫，

蓬莱洞。

青松影里，

红藕香中。

千机云锦重，

一片银河冻。

缥缈佳人双飞凤，

紫箫寒月满长空。

阑干晚风，

菱歌上下，

渔火西东。

品读

　　这首散曲写黄昏到夜静的西湖景色，虚实相生，明暗交替，浓丽清幽相映相衬，构成了一个奇幻美丽的艺术世界。"蕊珠宫，蓬莱洞"，散曲一开篇就把读者引入一种神奇的想象，黄昏的西湖，光影朦胧，仿佛已超离了凡尘的世界。"青松影里，红藕香中"，树影森森，荷香浮动，松的苍翠劲拔与荷的红艳明丽相互映衬。"千机云锦重，一片银河冻"，一天霞辉，如千机云锦披挂天空，锦绣斑斓，转瞬消退，只剩一片平滑如镜的湖水，倒映天光，如银河封冻。"缥缈佳人双飞凤，紫箫

寒月满长空"，清凉的湖面上，晚风传来一阵美妙的箫声，渺渺茫茫，
让人生出浪漫的想象，月光里仿佛有乘风的仙人双双飞过天空。这时的
诗人，凭倚在湖亭的栏杆上，享受着送爽的晚风，聆听着菱歌的起落，
眼瞅着渔火点点闪动，真不知身处天上还是人间。

Tune: Universal Joy

The West Lake

Zhang Kejiu

The pearly palace hall,

The Penglai Fairy cave.

In the shade of the green pines tall

Wafts the fragrance of red lotus blooms.

Sunset glow with cloud woven in brocade,

Like frozen Silver River in the boundless sky.

The ethereal beauty flies in the wind with phoenix wings,

The tune of a vertical bamboo flute (XIAO) chill the moon in the night.

The evening breeze caresses the balustrade,

Lotus girl's songs waft low and high,

Fishermens lanterns float east and west, far and nigh.

Literary Appreciation

This song poem writes about the picturesque landscape of the West Lake during the transition from dusk to nightfall. The harmonious coexistence of the virtual and the real, the alternation between light and dark, and the juxtaposition of beauty and tranquility collectively form an extraordinary and aesthetically pleasing art piece. Through "Pearly Palace, Penglai Cave", this song poem introduced readers to a captivating and enchanting portrayal of a fantastical world. During the twilight hours, the West Lake exudes an ethereal ambiance, as the interplay of dim lights and shadows imbues it with otherworldly allure. Meanwhile, "in the shade of the green pines tall, wafts the fragrance of red lotus blooms" depict a scene whereby the dense shadows cast by the verdant pines create a contrasting backdrop for the vibrant, radiant, and fragrant lotus blossoms. The next sentences, "sunset glow with cloud woven in brocade, like frozen Silver River in the boundless sky", portray the magnificent sunglow that resembles a cluster of clouds suspended in the sky. However, its brilliance diminishes rapidly, leaving behind a serene lake that mirrors the sky and is as splendid as the galaxy. Meanwhile, "the ethereal beauty flies in the wind, the tune of a vertical bamboo flute (XIAO) chill the moon in the night", paint the enchanting resonance of the bamboo flute one can experience in the serene, cook lake. As the evening breeze gently blows, the melodious notes of the flute permeate the air, evoking a sense of boundless beauty and prompting romantic imagination, such as the deities flying across the sky under the moonlight. The writer, in this moment, found solace by resting against the railing of the pavilion in the middle of the lake, enjoying the refreshing evening breeze, while immersing himself in the melodious tunes of the bamboo flutes and the flickering lights emitting from fishing boats, which is an experience as heavenly as one could possibly imagine.

山坡羊

闺思

张可久

云松螺髻,

香温鸳被,

掩春闺一觉伤春睡。

柳花飞,

小琼姬,

一声雪下呈祥瑞。

团圆梦儿生唤起。

谁,

不做美?

呸,

却是你!

品读

春日迟迟,闺门深掩,伤春的少妇恹恹而睡。柳絮漫空飘飞,美丽的小丫头被引动了天真的诗趣,在她眼中飘飘扬扬的柳絮都幻化成了白雪,一声欢快的"雪下呈祥瑞",不料却将女主人从"团圆梦儿"里生生唤起,温馨旖旎刹那成泡影,不由她又恼又气:"谁,不做美?"发觉是不晓事的小丫头,一腔恼恨又无从排解:"呸,却是你!"恨声责怪,说尽了怅惘与无奈。

　　一首小令却包含了一场戏剧冲突，甚至写入了女主人的言辞声气。两位出场人物对比生动，形象鲜明，气氛情境逼真如见。作者艺术手腕之高超，于此可见一斑。

Tune: Sheep on Mountain Slope

A Wife Bored

Zhang Kejiu

Her hair loose as cloud,

Her lovebirds quilt with fragrance overflowed in bed.

Her boudoir closed, shes deep in vernal sleep.

Willow down flies,

Her young maid cries:

"Oh! What auspicious snow!"

It wakes her from the dream of her love she will keep.

"Who

What a bore!"

Oh,

"It is you!"

Literary Appreciation

The arrival of spring has been delayed, the door to the boudoir is tightly shut, and the young woman, saddened by the delayed spring, is feeling sleepy. The air was filled with catkins, which inspired a lovely young maid. In her eyes, the catkins were a blanket of white snow, and her exclaims of "what auspicious snow!" woke the young woman from her "reunite dream", causing the warmth and love felt in the dream to abruptly dissipate and irritating her, as evident by "Who, What a bore!" When the young woman found out that it was the young maid who did not know better, the young woman could only struggle to suppress her anger, exclaiming "Oh, it's you!" At first glance, she castigated the young maid, but in fact, she is expressing her disappointment and powerlessness.

This song poem encompasses a compelling dramatic conflict and vividly portrays the profile of the young woman with dynamic settings; the two characters in question exhibit a striking contrast, presenting distinct images. It is an embodiment of the writer's exceptional artistic abilities.

一枝花

湖上归

张可久

（一）一枝花

长天落彩霞，

远水涵秋镜。

花如人面红，

山似佛头青。

　生色围屏，

翠冷松云径，

　嫣然眉黛横。

但携将旖旎浓香，

何必赋横斜瘦影。

（二）梁州

挽玉手留连锦英，

据胡床指点银瓶。

素娥不嫁伤孤另。

　想当年小小，

　问何处卿卿。

　东坡才调，

　西子娉婷，

总相宜千古留名。

吾二人此地私行，

六一泉亭上诗成。

三五夜花前月明，

十四弦指下风生。

可憎，

有情，

捧红牙合和伊州令。

万籁寂，

四山静，

幽咽泉流水下声，

鹤怨猿惊。

（三）尾

岩阿禅窟鸣金磬，

波底龙宫漾水精。

夜色清，

酒力醒。

宝篆销，

玉漏鸣。

笑归来仿佛二更，

煞强似踏雪寻梅，

灞桥冷。

品读

这是一套享誉极高的散曲，明人李开先推为"古今绝唱"，沈德符也把它和马致远的《夜行船·秋思》并列为"一时绝唱"，今人多认为两曲分别代表了元散曲豪放和清丽两种风格。

全套曲词写作者携美人游西湖，指点湖山、流连风月、赋诗听琴的雅逸情趣。曲中景色清妙，辞旨婉约放逸，且善糅前人名诗意境入曲，典雅蕴藉，音韵悠扬，不愧前人盛誉。

全曲分三个部分。《一枝花》一曲写黄昏西湖美景，设色鲜明，造境清幽，人物风流，意趣不俗。《梁州》写携手同游，饮酒赏花，两情相洽，泉畔赋诗，月下听琴；时间从黄昏渐入深夜，"万籁寂，四山静"，人心自得，欢愉恬静。《尾》曲写夜阑酒醒，尽兴归来，怡然自乐。夜半佛寺钟磬，水中亭合倒影，奇幻迷人，那种酒醒犹存的余兴，直透人心。

古人不满现实，多归隐田园，寄兴湖山，诗酒遣情，但也有混迹市尘、放浪形骸，如李白所谓"载妓随波任去留"，或杜收"十年一觉扬州梦"者，虽然表现不同，却殊途同归。元代文人，多仕途坎坷，无意功名，醉心林泉者和混迹勾栏者，都大有人在，张小山此曲，可以说将两条路并到了一起。还需注意的是，曲中对待同游之人的态度，这已不是纯然玩弄的狎昵，而是两情相悦的雅意；这是历史的一个进步，也是此曲格调高雅不俗的地方。

Tune: A Sprig of Flowers

Return from the Lake

Zhang Kejiu

(I) Tune: A Sprig of Flowers

Rainbow clouds fall from endless sky,

The lake covered with scenery of the Autumn.

The flowers coloured like the glowing face,

The mountains greened in deep.

Above all is colored screen,

Roadside pines in cold emerald dye,

The green mountains are very beautiful.

Coming with my love fair and tender,

Need I envy plum blossoms sweet and slender?

(II) Tune: Song of Frontier

I linger amid flowers, holding her soft hands,

And drink in silver cup, sitting in cozy chair.

The Moon Goddess, leaving her lover, lonely appears.

I think of the famous Geisha named Su xiaoxiao,

Who is her lover now accompanying her declining years?

My brilliant talent as famous poet Su dongpo,

Together with the lady as beautiful fairy.

Wish both we are can be remembered by the descendant.

I come here with my lover at leisure,

We write poems by fountain side with pleasure.

On the fifteenth night of the lunar calendar,

The flowers, the moon and the Chinese Zither playing,

How lovely they seem!

Her ivory clappers accompany her song of tune name.

The night tranquil,

All mountains still,

We hear the fountain sob with running stream,

The monkey cry

And the crane sigh

(Ⅲ) Tune: Epilogue

The golden bowl knocking in rocky temple,

The crystal palace reflected on the lake.

Night air fresh turned,

From wine I wake.

The incense burned,

Water clock sings.

When we come back in happy, it seems midnight or after.

Is it not better than to go

To seek plum blossom flowers on the bridge cold with snow?

Literary Appreciation

This collection of song poems was endorsed by Li Kaixian of the Ming dynasty as a "masterpiece of ancient and modern times", and alongside Ma Zhiyuan's *Double Tune*, *Nocturnal Boat*, *Fall Miss*, honored a "masterpiece of the times" by Shen Defu. At present, many believe that the two song poems each exemplify the unbridled and aesthetic styles of Yuan Qu.

This collection of song poems describes the writer's journey to West Lake with a woman, during which he highlighted the refined allure of the lakes and mountains, indulged in the gentle breeze and moonlight, and composed poems while appreciating the melodies of the qin. It also showcases a vivid and captivating scenery, with its graceful and mellow rhetoric, and effectively reflects the artistic conception found in famous poems of the past that are elegant and melodious, which truly lives up to the esteemed reputation of its predecessors.

This collection consists of three song poems. The first is set to the tune of *A Sprig of Flowers*, writing about the beautiful scenery of the West Lake at dusk, vividly portraying the bright colors, serene landscapes, romantic characters, and their harmonious interactions. The second song poem is set to the tune of the *Song of Frontier*, writing a journey with a companion, during which they drank and appreciated the flowers, exchanged feelings, composed poems by the spring, and listened to qin's melodious tones under the moonlit sky. From dusk until late night, people are contented, pleased, and serene, as exemplified by the phrase "all is quiet, all the mountains are quiet". Whereas the third and last song poem is the epilogue; it portrays the middle of the night, when the speaker sobers from the drinking earlier, and enjoys the resonant chimes of the Buddhist temple that reverberate through the air. The surrounding pavilions also create a mesmerizing visual effect as their reflections are inverted in the tranquil waters of the lake, which is amplified by the lingering effect of the wine to leave an impression on the speaker, evoking a deep emotional response.

Most of the ancients expressed discontentment with the society through reclusion to the countryside, shifting their focus on everyday life and poems and wine. However, there were also people who embraced life in the city and indulged in excessive and rather immoral behavior. For example, Li Bai's practice of "taking courtesan to stay with the waves" and Du Fu's "occasional dreaming of Yangzhou", despite distinct expressions, tell the same tale. During the Yuan dynasty, many scholar−officials experienced various challenges throughout their careers and displayed a lack of interest in fame and influence. Instead, they were deeply engrossed in a desire for seclusion or indulged in excessive behavior. Therefore, this collection of song poems is a combination of these two distinct styles. It should also be noted that the portrayal of the female character in these song poems is not merely a flirtatious encounter, but rather a depiction of two people who share similar qualities. This development holds significance within the context of poetry's portrayal of female characters, serving as a notable example of the song's sophisticated style.

蟾宫曲

春情

徐再思

平生不会相思，

才会相思，

便害相思。

身似浮云，

心如飞絮，

气若游丝。

空一缕余香在此，

盼千金游子何之？

证候来时，

正是何时？

灯半昏时，

月半明时。

品读

平白如话的诗句，将相思情状刻画得细微曲折，入肌入理。

从曲词看，害相思的该是一位有钱人家的少妇，丈夫出门远游，妻子独守空闺。本来是"闺中少妇不知愁"（王昌龄《闺怨》），也许是"春日凝妆上翠楼"（王昌龄《闺怨》），陌头青青的杨柳，使她春心顿醒，思情陡起，"才会相思，便害相思"，竟至"身似浮云，心如飞絮，气若游丝"，神情恍惚，坐卧不宁，相思成疾。"空一缕余香在此，盼千金游子何之"，最见少妇思夫本色。《古诗十九首》有"荡子行不归，空床难独守"，曹丕《燕歌行》有"君何淹留寄他方，贱妾茕茕守空房"，诗意大体相同，而此曲更为自然平易。"空一缕余香在此"，丈夫的身体气味仿佛还留在闺中，但他人呢？真让人思念呀，一掷千金的他，此刻又在哪里呢？思念中又掺入了一点忧虑。相思病何时最剧？自然是夜阑人静，"灯半昏时，月半明时"，这样的时辰本该是夫妻相对、欢爱情洽的时刻，但对独守空闺的她，这时的况味却最难言说。

Tune: Song of Moon Palace

Lovesickness

Xu Zaisi

In early life I knew nothing about sickness of love,

When I began to know a bit,

I fell heart and soul into a fit.

My body like floating clouds,

My heart like willow down in flight,

I feel completely exhausted.

In vain a wreath of fragrance is left here.

When will my noble lover come back?

When comes my sickness,

Can I know what time it is?

It comes by dim lamplight

When the moon is half bright.

Literary Appreciation

The portrayal of lovesickness in this song poem with simple and everyday language is characterized by intricate and nuanced elements. Based on the lyrics, this song poem depicts a young woman hailing from a privileged background who is suffering from lovesickness, as her husband has embarked on a long trip, leaving her behind. At first, "a young woman in a boudoir has no worries" and "puts on makeup to go out during spring" (Wang Changling's *A*

Young Woman's Sorrow）. However, as the poem progresses, she sees the green willows, which remind her of her sorrow. It is at this point "only she begins to experience lovesickness" and "her heart and soul fall into a fit"; even "her body like a floating cloud, her heart as light as willow down, and she is left utterly exhausted". The young woman is entranced, restless, and lovesick, and the true essence of lovesickness is encapsulated by the phrase "In vain a wreath of fragrance is left here, When will my noble lover come back?" Furthermore, it is stated in the *Nineteen Ancient Poems* that "I can't stay alone in an empty bed if you don't return", and in Cao Pi's *Song of Yan* that "he stays for a long time to enjoy another party, and a disrespecting concubine stays in the empty room", They both convey messages similar to that from this song poem, but this song poem has a more natural and effortless style. The phrase "in vain a wreath of fragrance is left here" depicts a scene where the young woman's husband's scent lingers in the boudoir, although he had been gone for a while. Her longing for his company is accompanied by a slight concern, as he is known for his philanthropic nature. Notably, this song poem effectively captures the nature of lovesickness, which is the most severe during quiet nights, exemplified by the phrase "it comes by dim lamplight, when the moon is half bright", as this time is typically the time the husband and wife spend together, happily and very in love. However, the young woman finds herself in an empty boudoir, evoking emotions beyond description.

水仙子

夜雨

徐再思

一声梧叶一声秋，

一点芭蕉一点愁，

三更归梦三更后。

落灯花，棋未收，

叹新丰孤馆人留。

枕上十年事，

江南二老忧，

都到心头。

品读

夜雨思乡是诗文表现的一个老话题，但在不同作家的笔下，它能构造出不同的艺术境界。徐再思这一支散曲就以逼真如画的描摹和深沉浑厚的情思，在古今同类杰作中别辟一域。

"一声梧叶一声秋，一点芭蕉一点愁，三更归梦三更后"，是秋天的雨夜，雨滴打在宽阔的梧叶、芭蕉上，敲出一种单调、凄清的节奏，诱人进入回家的梦，又将人从梦里唤回，梦回时节，恰是夜静人寂的三更过后，此刻，雨滴声听来就更添了一种凉意，一些忧愁。睁眼看看室内的一切，"落灯花，棋未收，叹新丰孤馆人留"，残烛尚明，凌乱的棋盘无言地诉说着睡前寂寥落寞的心情，一种潦倒失意、漂泊寄居的惨淡催人叹息。头倚枕上，十年来悲欢离合的无数旧事，掺和着思念家乡的父母，担心他们的安康的忧思，乱麻麻一齐逼上心头。这一夜合该是眼睁睁到天明了吧，不独作者，读者也能感受到那一种令人鼻酸的气息。

　　这支曲还有一个地方值得注意，这就是数词在曲中的巧妙应用。"一声梧叶一声秋，一点芭蕉一点愁"，重复出现的数词，直观地表现出雨打阔叶时的单调节奏，但曲词本身却不因之单调，反倒有一种悠长舒徐的格调。"枕上十年事，江南二老忧"，"十"与"二"相对，句式对偶，精警而和谐。

Tune: Song of Daffodils

Rainy Night

Xu Zaisi

I hear autumn's sigh in a plane's fading leaf,

I see raindrops on bananas as drops of grief.

After midnight I dream of home-coming at midnight,

The candle was still bright, and the messy chess still in chessboard,

How can a frustrated and losing man in an inn not sigh?

Ten years like a dream on the pillow pass by,

Old parents far apart in hometown,

Now come into my heart

Literary Appreciation

The theme of homesickness on a rainy night has been a recurring subject in poetry throughout history. However, it can be skillfully explored through the different artistic approaches taken by various writers. In this song poem, the writer has made significant contributions to the realm of literary master-pieces, both in ancient and modern times, and carved a niche within this genre through his use of vivid and picturesque descriptions, as well as his a-bility to convey deep and vigorous emotions.

The first three sentences depict the scene of a rainy autumn night. The raindrops hit the wide leaves and plantains, producing a repetitive and melan-cholic pattern, which entices people to slumber to dream of returning home,

115

while simultaneously waking them, interrupting their dreams. It is just after midnight when people are awakened, and the raindrops add to the chilliness. The speaker opens their eyes and look at the surroundings within the room, and they notice that "the candle was still bright, and the messy chess still in chessboard; how can a frustrated and losing man in an inn not sigh". The still−bright candle and the disorganized chess shuttlecock wordlessly conveyed a sense of solitude before the speaker rested for the night, exuding the frustration and the desolate nature of traveling and sojourning, which often elicit sighs from the speaker. As they lean on the pillow, a multitude of old stories, encompassing both joys and sorrows from the past decade, intertwine with the sentiments of longing for their parents and hometown and expressing concern for their loved ones' well−being unfold. It's the dawn of the night.

The writer had portrayed such a scene that share the emotional response that evokes tears with the readers, particularly through the ingenious application of numerals in the lines, "A sigh in a leaf, raindrops on banana as drops of grief." The repeated numerals intuitively show the repetitive rhythm created by raindrops falling on broad leaves. However, despite this monotony, the lyrics themselves maintain a lengthy and calming style. This application of numerals can also be seen in the phrases "Ten years like a dream on the pillow pass by, two old parents far apart in hometown", which created a contrast between the numbers "ten" and "two". This juxtaposition is a perfect example of antithesis, and is unequivocal yet balanced.

解三醒
真氏

奴本是明珠擎掌，

怎生的流落平康？

对人前乔做作娇模样，

背地里泪千行。

三春南国怜飘荡，

一事东风没主张。

添悲怆，

那里有珍珠十斛，

来赎云娘！

品读

关于这支小令，有一个故事。姚燧任翰林学士时，在一次宴会上遇到一个歌妓，自称是名儒真德秀后人，父亲在朔方做官时，因禄薄侵贷公帑，无力偿还，被卖入娼家。姚燧同情她的遭遇，便替她赎了身，后真氏改嫁一小史。故事见于《辍耕录》，但其间并无此曲，因而有人怀疑它出自后人伪托。不过，这支曲写妓女生活的痛苦，甚为真切，尤其是以第一人称的泣诉口吻写出，愈加感人。

一个良家女子，自幼父母视若掌上明珠，但喜欢捉弄人的命运却将她推入了烟花柳巷，"对人前乔做作娇模样，背地里泪千行"，那一种痛苦辛酸，真是难于言表；而更使她感觉人生无望的是，那种飘零无着的处境，"三春南国怜飘荡，一事东风没主张"，这样的日子什么时候才是个头呢？结尾三句，是渺茫无望的呼号。这样的曲词，若无真实的人生体验，恐怕难以假托得出。

Tune：Thrice Drunk and Sobered

Maiden ofZhen Family

I was a precious pearl in my parents' palm

How could I strand in this place?

Pretend to be charming in front of man,

And tears thousands of lines behind them.

Homeless for three years, far from the southern land,

When will this day end?

Im further grieved,

To find someone can pay a lot of pearls for me,

That I may be relieved.

Literary Appreciation

This song poem is based on a story. During Yao Sui's tenure as a Hanlin academician, he crossed paths with a courtesan at a banquet who claimed to be a descendant of a famous Confucian scholar, Zhen Dexiu. She was sold to the brothel by her father, then an official in Shuofang, who failed to repay the public funds he embezzled. Yao sympathized with her sufferings, and hence paid the price for her release from the brothel. Later, she married a man holding an inferior title in the government. This story can be located within the Notes on Farming in the South, but there is no song poem by that name during that time. Therefore, some suspect that it may have originated from a misguid-

119

ed belief by the later generations. Despite itsunverifiable origin, this song poem portraying the hardships of a courtesan's life is remarkably realistic, particularly due to its poignant first – person narrative and emotive tone, which further enhances its impact and emotional resonance.

The courtesan discussed in this song poem was once an educated young lady cherished by her parents throughout her upbringing, but fate played a hand, and she ended up in the brothel. She "pretends to be charming in front of man", and sheds "tears thousands of lines behind them"; the hardships she faces and the emotions she experiences are beyond words. Adding to her sense of hopelessness is the fact that she has no control of her own self, as evidenced by the concluding sentences of this song poem, portraying the speaker's desperate cries. This intense emotion that reflects real–life experiences can be challenging to be accurately captured in lyricism.

清江引

秋居

吴西逸

白雁乱飞秋似雪，
清露生凉夜。
扫却石边云，
醉踏松根月，
星斗满天人睡也。

品读

《秋居》描绘的是一位深山逸士的秋夜生活图景。"白雁乱飞秋似雪"一句，像一幅淡雅的中国画，画面上有群飞的白雁，也有水滨扬花放白的芦荻，不待看到"清露生凉夜"，那一片皑皑似雪的色泽就使人真切地感受到一丝秋的凉意。"扫却石边云，醉踏松根月"，画面移到了高山林径，居于"白云生处"，石边便常有白色的云雾缭绕。"扫却石边云"一句令人浮想联翩，如何"扫"？是衣袂不经意的拂开，还是真拿了一件麈尾之类的器物去扫？总之这一句已使人恍若置身仙境；"醉踏松根月"更添了一种悠然飘逸的神韵。不过，最美的还是最后一句："星斗满天人睡也"，多么自在逍遥，多么闲适静美，那真该是梦里才有的仙境。对生活在现代都市灰白夜晚中的人们，那真该是梦里才有的仙境。

Tune: Song of Clear River

An Autumn Night

Wu Xiyi

White wild geese fly up and down like snow in autumn,

Clear dew-drops grow in the cool night.

Drunk, I tread on the pine trees' root in moonlight,

Sweeping away the cloud on the edge of the stone,

Under the starry sky sleepy I lie.

Literary Appreciation

The Autumn Night describes the ambiance of an autumn night within a secluded mountain setting. The phrase "white wild geese fly up and down like snow in autumn" bears resemblance to a simple and elegant Chinese painting depicting flocks of white geese in flight, accompanied by flourishing reeds along the waterfront. From the white reeds alone, the speaker can feel the autumn's coolness, even though it is not yet the time of the year for "clear dew and cool night" . Then, through the phrases "Sweeping away the cloud on the edge of the stone, Drunk, I tread on the pine trees' root in moonlight", the imagery transitions to mountains and trails, where the speaker resides amidst the "above and deep clouds" and often sees white clouds encircling the stones. The act of "sweeping away the cloud on the edge of the stone" evokes interests among readers; they can not help but wonder if the clouds are accidentally brushed aside by the speaker's clothes, or does the speaker intentionally use a dust-whisk or similar tool to achieve the goal? Meanwhile, the phrase "drunk, I tread on the pine trees' root in moonlight" adds a leisurely ambiance to this song poem. Nevertheless, the most intriguing aspect of this song poem lies within the last sentence, which effectively paints the speaker's carefree and leisure life. For people living within the mundane urban landscapes of modern cities, the imagery presented in this song poem evoke a sense of familiarity akin to their wildest dreams.

普天乐

嘲西席

张鸣善

讲诗书，

习功课。

爹娘行孝顺，

兄弟行谦和。

为臣要尽忠，

与朋友休言过。

养性终朝端然坐，

免教人笑俺风魔。

先生道学生琢磨，

学生道先生絮聒，

馆东道不识字由他。

品读

这是一出颇耐寻味的喜剧，三个出场人物，先生的迂腐、学生的刁顽、家长的放任，形成鲜明的对照，一种世态人心，一种旧教育制度的痼疾，昭然若揭。

先生是一个既可笑又让人同情的角色，看他成天教导学生的内容，我们就可以想象出他有怎样一副板正僵硬的面容。他所讲的，按那个时代的标准来说，都是人生"至理"，但这些"至理"本身却缺少一种人所必需的生气，再加上僵死的灌输式教学，他就将自己推上了一种十分尴尬的境地。学生对他的反感，应该说是有几分理由的，让人对他产生同情的是家长的态度。无论如何，先生还是忠于职守的，但在他眼里神圣的一切，在那有钱的家长看来，却是可有可无，这就真让人有点哭笑不得，不知该嘲弄的是先生那死板的方式，还是那认真负责的态度。

这支曲的艺术价值是该得到高评价的，直到今天，它还可以是做"先生"的人的一面镜子。

Tune: Universal Joy

To a Funny Tutor

Zhang Mingshan

You teach pupils to read and write,

And they learn to recite,

To obey their fathers and mothers,

To be modest and polite for their brothers,

To be loyal to their king till the end,

And not to find fault with their friend.

Well bred, you make a pose all the day long,

Nobody should say you are wrong.

You tell the pupils: "Your work should be well done."

But they say: "The work is a tedious one."

And the father says: "All is up to my son."

Literary Appreciation

This comedy is captivating as it presents a distinct contrast between the pedantic nature of the teacher, the stubbornness of the students, and the laissez-faire attitude of the parents, revealing the significant and severe problem in the old education system.

The teacher is a laughable yet pitiful character. Just from the subject matter he teaches his students throughout the day, one can imagine his stern face. Based on the prevailing standards of that time period, his teachings were considered to be the "truth" of life. However, these "truths" lacked needed vitality, and due to his inflexible teaching methods, he found himself in an awkward predicament. It is worth noting that what without a reason is not the students' dislike of him, but rather the demeanor of the students' parents towards him. In any case, the teacher demonstrates unwavering commitment to fulfilling his duties, and what holds immense value in his opinion is often deemed expendable by affluent parents. This stark contrast between perspectives elicits a range of emotions, evoking both amusement and sorrow; therefore, the imagery presented may lead to confusion among readers regarding whether the teacher's inflexible teaching methodology or his earnest and accountable demeanor is the subject of ridicule.

This song poem should receive higher artistic merit than it warrants. Until today, it can serve as a medium for educators to reflect upon themselves.

水仙子

西湖探梅

杨朝英

雪晴天地一冰壶，

竟往西湖探老逋，

骑驴踏雪溪桥路。

笑王维作画图，

拣梅花多处提壶。

对酒看花笑，

无钱当剑沽，

醉倒在西湖。

品读

本曲写诗人雪霁踏雪寻梅时的情景，潇洒豪迈，颇见闲逸生活情趣。

"雪晴天地一冰壶"，此喻颇见气魄，也颇具奇巧，湖山的晶莹皎洁和胸怀的清明澄澈，同时显现在读者眼前；"竟往西湖探老逋，骑驴踏雪溪桥路"，是探梅路雪时情景的写真，但高士襟怀也于中隐隐透出，情境的直接言说当然是最主要的，但"老逋""骑驴"这些能引人联想的语词的暗示作用也不可忽略。"老逋"是梅，亦是一种人格精神，"骑驴"是行脚方式，但早已浸淫着极浓的文化情韵，我们可以从之联想到李白的骑驴过华阴、孟浩然的灞陵赏梅、李贺的骑驴吟诗、陆游的剑门遇雨……而所有的联想都加强着诗人此举的风雅味。"笑王维

作画图，拣梅花多处提壶"，对着湖山美景，诗人心底涌起一股豪情，
王维作画不知画得出如此天然美景否？无论如何，此刻移情于画有点辜
负当前，还是醉酒花荫更加惬意。"对酒看花笑，无钱当剑沽，醉倒在
西湖"，诗人的喜悦已近癫狂，也更显痛快淋漓。

Tune：Song of Daffodils

Mume Blossoms at West Lake

Yang Chaoying

The sky and earth look like icy pot after snow,

To seek after plum blossom in West Lake I go,

To tread on snow brook trail by donkey I ride.

Laughing at Wang Wei's painting picture of the lakeside,

I bring a pot of wine where plum blossoms.

Wine cup in hand, I smile at the flowers for long,

Wine drunk up, I may pawn my sword to buy,

Drunk down, by lakeside I would lie.

Literary Appreciation

This song poem describes the writer's experience during heavy snow weather in search of the plum blossom, and is characterized by its natural, unbridled, and bold style, while implying thepleasure in leisure life.

The metaphor "The sky and earth look like icy pot after snow" is a verve and ingenious expression of the crystal clear lakes and mountains, complemented by the evident ambition that is presented to readers at the same time. Meanwhile, "To seek after plum blossom in West Lake I go, To tread on snow brook trail by donkey I ride" captures the serene beauty of searching for the plum blossom on the snowy road, while subtly revealing the scholar's intellect. On the other hand, although it is important to explicitly represent the imagery, it is also imperative to acknowledge the implicit connotations, such as *laobu* and the donkey rode. In this context, *laobu* refers to the plum blossom and a unique characteristic of a person, whereas a donkey ride is a transportation means that has been ingrained in Chinese culture, thereby possessing a significant cultural allure. The mentioned instances include Li Bai's journey on a donkey through Huayin, Meng Haoran's admiration of plum blossom in Baling, Li He's recitation of songs and poems while riding a donkey, and Lu You's encounter with rainfall at the Jianmen Pass. These associations reinforce the refined artistry of the poet's behavior to "laugh at Wang Wei's painting picture of the lakeside", and "bring a pot of wine where plum blossoms". As the writer gazed upon the beautiful scenery of lakes and mountains, pride filled his heart, believing that Wang Wei could not possibly accurately depict the inherent beauty of nature through his paintings. At that moment, he realized that it might not be entirely appropriate to think about a painting, but instead, he should indulge in wine and be drunk. "Wine cup in hand, I smile at the flowers for long; Wine drunk up, I may pawn my sword to buy; Drunk down, by lakeside I would lie." From these sentences, it is evident that the writer's exuberant joy is almost bordering on madness, which adds to its captivating nature.

山坡羊

道情

宋方壶

青山相待，

白云相爱，

梦不到紫罗袍共黄金带。

一茅斋，

野花开，

管甚谁家兴废谁成败，

陋巷箪瓢亦乐哉！

贫，气不改；

达，志不改。

品读

这是作者的言志之作，表达了他甘居林下，不因贫贱、显达改节的崇高精神。

"青山相待，白云相爱，梦不到紫罗袍共黄金带"一句，将隐居生活写得十分安闲惬意，青山、白云两句，拟人写出，既描景又传情，作者是真正陶醉于自然美景之中的，连"梦"也不与那些功名富贵沾一沾边。"一茅斋，野花开，管甚谁家兴废谁成败，陋巷箪瓢亦乐哉"开头两句，具体写出自己山居的环境，接着抒发不问世事、安于清贫的思想，似乎很旷达、很看得开，其实还是内心对现实政治不满的流露，看一看他在明初写的《斗鹌鹑·送别》的结尾："庆风调雨顺升平日，保一统江山社稷。托赖着千千载仁主圣明朝，齐仰贺万万岁吾皇大明国"，就能懂得，所谓"管甚谁家兴废谁成败"不过是不满于元末动乱的话。"贫，气不改；达，志不改"，曲末两句写得很是掷地有声，其思想也还是孟子所谓"贫贱不能移""富贵不能淫"的翻版，但若真能做到，那也就足称"大丈夫"了。

Tune: Sheep on Mountain Slope

A Carefree Dream

Song Fanghu

Green hills treat each other in peace,

White clouds hold each other in love,

I can't dream of a golden belt in purple robes.

Only living a thatched room,

With wild flowers in blooming,

Careless alike of rise and fall, of failure and success.

In simple food and plain living I'll find delight

Even if poor, ambition will not change.

Even if rich, ambition will not change.

Literary Appreciation

This song poem exemplifies the writer's ambition, reflecting his lofty inclination towards living in seclusion and remaining steadfast in his morals, regardless of his financial situation.

It begins by describing the comfort the writer experienced in his seclusion; "green hills" and "white clouds" are personified to depict scenic landscapes while also conveying his fondness of the lifestyle. Through this song poem, he expressed a profound appreciation for the inherent allure of nature, and even his "dream" is free of any association with fame and wealth. The phrases "A thatched room, wild flowers bloom, regardless of who will succeed or fail, In simple food and plain living I'll find delight" depict the surroundings of the writer's personal dwelling situated in the mountains. Then, he proceeded to convey the apathy towards worldly matters and content with a state of poverty, which may initially appear open-minded, but on second thought, it reveals a political discontent. This sentiment is also evident in the concluding lines of the writer's work in the early Ming dynasty, Tone: Playing Quails An Outing, where he states, "Celebrate the good weather and keep the country unified; Thanks to empires benevolent rule of the Ming Dynasty generation and generation", which allow us to understand that the concept of "success or decay regardless of the family's prosperity or failure" arises from the dissatisfaction caused by the unrest during the final years of the Yuan dynasty.

The concluding sentences of this song poem, "Even if poor, ambition will not change; Even if rich, ambition will not change", reflect Mencius' ideology that neither riches nor honors can corrupt him, and neither poverty nor abasement can make him swerve from his principles. However, this feat is quite impossible; if accomplished, one can be honored as the man of noble character.

清江引

托咏

宋方壶

剔秃圞一轮天外月，

拜了低低说：

是必常团圆，

休着些儿缺，

愿天下有情底都似你者。

品读

　　此曲借托少女拜月祝辞，故题《托咏》。主题从《西厢记》"愿天下有情的都成了眷属"脱胎而来，但更见形象生动。拜月的情景有着浓郁的民俗风情美，主人公的言辞声气逼肖真实，整支曲仿佛是一个优美爱情故事的一段精彩细节。艺术构思方式源自冯廷巳《长命女》："春日宴，绿酒一杯歌一遍，再拜陈三愿：一愿郎君千岁，二愿妾身常健，三愿如同梁上燕，岁岁长相见。"但更通俗平易，也更具生活真实和艺术感染力。

Tune: Song of Clear River

To the Moon

Song Fanghu

So round is the full moon in the sky.

The girl bows and whispers to her in view.

"You must be forever full on high,

And never wane to the eye!

I wish that those in love shall gather round as you. "

Literary Appreciation

This song poem is inspired by the reverence from a young girl who worships the moon, so it has been aptly named "To the Moon". Its central theme is the desire for all lovers in the world to be united in marriage, which is derived from the *Romance of the Western Chamber* and surpassed its original source in terms of expression. The moon worship ritual is rich in folk culture, and the key elements of the performance are characterized by their vibrant and authentic portrayal, culminating in a captivating narrative that beautifully depicts a tale of love. The artistic inspiration for this song poem is drawn from Feng Tingsi's *Long Life Girl*, in which a scene unfolds "at the spring feast, a cup of wine is drunk and a song is sung once again, and three wishes are made: I wish you a thousand years old, I wish myself a long and healthy life, and I wish that we are like flying swallows on the beam and we will be together forever". However, the artistic presentation is more straightforward and precisely executed in this song poem, in addition to its superb association with real life and quality.

醉高歌过红绣鞋

寄金莺儿

贾固

乐心儿比目连枝,

肯意儿新婚燕尔。

画船开抛闪的人独自,

遥望关西店儿。

黄河水流不尽心事,

中条山隔不断相思。

当记得夜深沉,

人静悄,

自来时。

来时节三两句话,

去时节一篇诗,

记在人心窝儿里直到死。

品读

据元末夏庭芝《青楼集》记载,贾固在山东任金宪时喜欢上了歌妓金莺儿,调赴西台御史后仍然不能忘情,就写了这支曲寄给她,并因此而遭上司弹劾罢官。这支曲的著名与这个浪漫故事当然大有关系,但即使不依附这个故事,就曲论曲,它也无愧于一流作品之名。

从回味当日共同生活的甜蜜,到自己离开后留给对方的孤独和思念,诗思巧妙,足见作者对金莺儿的深情与理解。写思念之情而从对方着笔，是古典诗词惯用的手法，贾固以之入曲，因了语言的贴近生活，更添了一份自然质朴。

　　"黄河水流不尽心事，中条山隔不断相思"工稳的对仗，将两道地理屏障变成了表现忠贞爱情的道具。接下来，曲意转向对当初交往细节的重温回味，情境气氛，使人恍若身临其境。最后一句"记在人心窝儿里直到死"，用民歌般的质朴语言，表现刻骨铭心的爱情，感人至深，将元曲的本色优势发挥得淋漓尽致。全曲无一语及于金莺儿容颜，纯写两情相悦，崇高脱俗。

From "Drinking Song" to "Embroidered Red Shoes"
For Golden Oriole
Jia Gu

Like flatfish or twin branches of a tree,

We were as happy as a pair of swallows free.

My painting boat left you alone on shore,

Gazing as far as west of the Sunny Pass.

Our love like Yellow River keeps on flowing,

The Middle Mountain can't bar it from growing.

Remember when night was deep,

All fell asleep,

You came alone.

Come, you spoke but two words or three;

Gone, you wrote a poem for me,

It would be kept in my heart till we are dead.

Literary Appreciation

According to Xia Tingzhi's Collection of Brothels published towards the end of the Yuan dynasty, Jia Gu developed romantic feelings for a courtesan named Jin Ying'er, after being appointed an official in Shandong Province, and could not erase her from his thoughts even after his transfer to serve as the procurator in Shanxi Province. Therefore, he composed a song poem dedicated to her and sent it accordingly. Regrettably, his actions led to his subsequent impeachment and dismissal. The popularity of this song poem is undeniably influenced by its romantic narrative, but even without considering the story behind it, the song poem itself is deserving of recognition as a top-tier piece of work.

The writer's deep affection for Jin is demonstrated through his ingenious poetic reflections, which range from the reminiscence of the delightful moments shared in their lives to the subsequent solitary and longing experienced upon parting ways. In classical poetry, it is a prevalent technique to portray the experience of lovesickness from the other's perspective. Using everyday language, the writer incorporated this technique in his song poem, leveraging its close association with everyday life, thereby enhancing the simplicity of this work.

"Our love like Yellow River keeps on flowing; the Middle Mountain can't bar it from growing." This consistent antithesis has turned the geographical barrier into symbolic representations of unwavering affection. Next, the song poem transitions into a reenactment of the details of their interactions, while the contextual ambiance creates an immersive setting for readers. The last sentence, "It would be kept in my heart till we are dead", conveys a profound affection using simple language comparable to those used in folk songs, effectively evoking emotional resonance and showcasing the inherent strengths of Yuan Qu. This song poem does not mention any details regarding Jin's physical attractiveness; rather, it focuses on the portrayal of the pair, which is a subline and refined artistic approach.

塞鸿秋

浔阳即景

周德清

长江万里白如练，

淮山数点青如淀。

江帆几片疾如箭，

山泉千尺飞如电。

晚云都变露，

新月初学扇，

塞鸿一字来如线。

品读

周德清是元曲作家中非常注重择字造句用韵的一位。他在《中原音韵》中强调，作曲宜"文而不文，俗而不俗，要耸观又耸听，格调高，音律好，衬字无，平仄稳"。从这首小令看，他在实践中也确是这么做的。这首《浔阳即景》，是作者在浔阳江头眺望四周景色的即兴之作，篇幅虽小，但内容极为丰富。它截取秋日傍晚云霞消散明月初升的一刻，将作者在江边的所见所感，编排选择，使景色的远近大小动静明暗对应并存，点、线、面交构，形成了一幅动态的立体景观，读后有身临其境之感。日落月升，云雾渐起，轻纱般飘浮着，远近青山如黛，流泉飞堕。浩渺来自天际的长江，似一匹巨大的白练，流动着，鼓荡着，往来穿行的帆船，在这澎湃的江面，只是几片帆叶，轻捷，快速。抬头之际，一行南归的鸿雁正从空中飞过，带着秋的凉意，带着边地的征尘，给这画面平添了一种苍凉雄浑之意。全曲七句，写了七景，而巧妙的比喻，使得这看似独立的七景有了生气，既对应又联系，字里行间也透露出作者的心境感受。七句中六句用韵，以紧锣密鼓的节奏，配合画面的辽远开阔，形成了激越雄壮的气势。

Tune: Autumn Swan on Frontier

By the River of Xunyang

Zhou Deqing

For miles and miles the endless Yangtze river flows silk-white;

Dots on dots color of southern hills stand indigo-blue.

Sails on sails go past as fast like arrows do.

The waterfall dashes down like lightning from the height.

All evening clouds turn into dew;

The crescent moon imitates a bow;

The wild geese from the frontier fly in a row.

Literary Appreciation

Zhou Deqing, a notable writer from the Yuan dynasty, demonstrated a keen focus on the careful selection of vocabulary, sentence construction, and the utilization of rhymes in his literary works. In his work titled the *Rhymes of the Central Plains*, he emphasized the importance of creating song poems that are "literary but not abscure, popular but not vulgar, and should be both sensational and breathtaking elegant style, good melody, no interlining, and smooth and steady". These requirements have been effectively implemented in this song poem.

By the River of Xunyang is an impromptu piece created by the writer while he looked at the picturesque surroundings near the upper reaches of the Xunyang River. Despite its brevity, the content of this song poem is remarkably comprehensive. The described imagery captures the precise instance when the clouds disperse and the luminous moon ascends in the autumn evening. It meticulously puts together the writer's observations and emotions experienced along the river, resulting in a work of art where the distant scenery, characterized by its liveliness and obscurity, converges with various elements such as points, lines, and surfaces. This convergence gives rise to a dynamic landscape, which allows the readers to feel as though they stand together with the writer. As the moon ascends, the clouds slowly ascend as well, drifting like delicate veils. The nearby and distant verdant hills take on an indigo shade, while the waterfalls soar through the air. At the same time, the expansive Yangtze River resembles a vast expanse of flowing white silk and satin, similar to a sailing boat, gracefully navigating the surging currents with only a few sails adorning its surface. As the writer gazes upwards, a formation of geese coming from the north traverses the sky, representing the autumn's arrival and dust from the border, contributing to the overall desolate yet robust essence conveyed by this scene. This song poem consists of seven scenes, each described in a single sentence. Through the use of clever metaphors, these seemingly disparate scenes come to life, creating a cohesive and interconnected imagery. The writer's mood and emotions are also subtly conveyed throughout the work. Out of the seven sentences, six use rhymes, exhibiting a pronounced rhythm and contributing to the creation of a captivating and grand momentum, characterized by the vast and distant picture.

醉太平
警世
汪元亨

憎苍蝇竞血，

恶黑蚁争穴。

急流中勇退是豪杰，

不因循苟且。

叹乌衣一旦非王谢，

怕青山两岸分吴越，

厌红尘万丈混龙蛇，

老先生去也。

品读

汪元亨生活的至正年间，正是元末社会变乱、群雄蜂起的时代，官场的黑暗、政治的腐败已使元王朝到了崩溃的边缘，农民起义和军阀混战加速着这一崩溃的进程，但同时也加深着生活在这一乱世的人民的苦难。汪元亨此曲流露出的思想，正是这一特定时代的产物。曲词前半四句，写他对仕宦生活的反感，及急流勇退、洁身自好的决心，态度鲜明，也比较单一；后半四句，一"叹"一"怕"一"厌"，则传达出了一种更加复杂的思想意绪，这里头有对社会巨变、人事沧桑的预感和体验，有对军阀割据、战乱频仍的忧惧，也有对纷扰争执、称王称霸局面的厌倦。"老先生去也"一句，看似洒脱，实则包含着很多的苦涩和无奈，和太平岁月的高言归隐有很大的不同。历来解此曲者，往往疏于此点，而这实在是不该疏忽的心理背景。

Tune: Drunk in Time of Peace

Disgust with the World

Wang Yuanheng

I hate flies striving to suck blood,

And black ants fighting for nest.

A brave man will retire at the high tide,

And not follow the old rut or drift along.

I sigh for mansions to lords no longer belong,

And fear blue hills into hostile states divide.

I dislike the secular society with all messing things,

As an old gentleman, I'll leave them with disgust.

Literary Appreciation

The peak of Wang Yuanheng's life coincided with a period characterized by societal turmoil and the rise of a select few great figures towards the end of the Yuan dynasty. The pervasive influence of bureaucracy and rampant political corruption had pushed the Yuan dynasty to the verge of collapse, a process expedited by the uprisings of farmers and the conflicts instigated by warlords. However, it is important to note that these events also exacerbated the hardships endured by the people during this tumultuous period. The ideas expressed by this writer in this song poem are a reflection of the prevailing sentiments of the era in which it was created. In the first four sentences of the song poem, he expressed his discontent towards his career as an official and his resolve to promptly retire and embrace amoral lifestyle. Through "sigh" "fear" and "disgust", the last four sentences convey the writer's more intricate and nuanced idea. There have been reports and accounts of significant societal shifts and fluctuations in daily life, and concerns have arisen regarding the rise of warlords, separatist regimes, and the prevalence of frequent conflicts. The phrase "As an old gentleman, I'll leave them with disgust" may initially appear carefree, but in actuality, it conveys an intense resentment and power-lessness, which starkly contrasts with the lofty notion of seclusion during peaceful times; the significance of this aspect is often overlooked by many who have analyzed this song poem, but it is precisely this aspect that holds the ut-most importance.

人月圆

倪瓒

惊回一枕当年梦，

　渔唱起南津。

　画屏云嶂，

　池塘春草，

　无限销魂。

　旧家应在，

　梧桐覆井，

　杨柳藏门。

　闲身空老，

　孤篷听雨，

　灯火江村。

品读

　　倪瓒中年弃家出走，泛舟五湖，颇见洒脱不羁，到晚年却不由得思恋起故乡来。这一曲《人月圆》，生动地描绘出他晚年江湖漂泊的生活情形，和寂寞、惆怅、凄凉的复杂心境。倪瓒是一位杰出的画家，人世沧桑的深沉况味，以历历如画的诗笔描出，更具一种荡气回肠的魅力。旅途梦醒，观览湖山，惊觉岁月的流逝，不觉思恋故乡，追怀往事，自伤孤零。这是一个真实具体的情境，但也有人生象征意味包孕其中。打动我们、感染我们的，除去倪瓒生活的传奇情味，更多的恐怕是这种"旅途梦醒"的人生感觉。

Tune: Man and Moon

Ni Zan

Startled on my pillow from my dream,

Remember fishing songs at southern stream

I see peak on peak veiled in clouds like a screen,

And pool on pool seem overgrown with grass green.

How much it grieves,

The thought kept going round and round in heart of my house.

Overshadowed by plane leaves.

With doors hidden amid willow trees.

At ease,

I am elder in vain.

What can I do but listen to the rain,

Or see flickering lights on river shore.

Literary Appreciation

Ni Zan ran away from his family during his middle years and travelled across the country. He was big-hearted and unruly, yet in his later years, he inevitably longed for his hometown. This song poem, titled *Man and Moon*, vividly portrays his nomadic life during his later years, along with his intricate emotional state characterized by feelings of solitude, sorrow, and isolation. The writer was also an exceptional painter renowned for his profound understanding and his refined taste in portraying the ever-changing nature of human life. Through his skillful use of language, he imbued his works with a captivating charm that evokes deep emotions. Throughout his journey, he awakened, embarked on journeys to lakes and mountains, and had a revelation upon reflecting on his past. This is when a deep yearning for his hometown emerged, accompanied by a longing for bygone days, filling him with feelings of solitude and despair. The song poem portrays a situation that is both concrete and symbolic, evoking the relatable experience of "waking up from a dream on a journey".

凭阑人

赠吴国良

倪瓒

客有吴郎吹洞箫，
明月沉江春雾晓。
湘灵不可招，
水云中环佩摇。

品读

　　吴国良是倪瓒一位善制墨又善吹箫的朋友，他这两样技艺都很得倪瓒嘉许，尤其是箫声，给漂泊寂寞中的倪瓒很大的心灵慰藉，此曲便为此而作。

　　"客有吴郎吹洞箫，明月沉江春雾晓"是写实的，但充满了艺术的妙趣。后一句既可看作是环境的描写，也可以看作是箫声在作者心中激发的想象，就如钟子期听伯牙弹琴而想到高山流水，空明迷蒙。"湘灵不可招，水云中环珮摇"两句，写箫声的感染力，用笔奇幻，浪漫绮丽，使人不禁想入非非。湘水的女神寻常当然是不可能被人招来的，但箫声也使她动情，水云中叮当的环佩声，该是她也在伫立凝听吧。

Tune: Leaning on Balustrade

For A Friend

Ni Zan

My friend is good at playing on the bamboo flute,

It may bring down the moon on misty stream in Spring,

Why can it not attract the fairy queen?

In cloud and water you may hear jade pendants ring.

Literary Appreciation

Wu Guoliang is a friend of Ni Zan who is proficient in the art of producing china ink as well as playing the bamboo flute, the two skills highly praised by Ni Zan, particularly his mastery of the bamboo flute. This melodious sound provides profound spiritual solace to Ni Zan, who often finds himself lost and alone. This song poem was written specifically for this purpose.

The first two sentences of this song poem are grounded in reality, and also carries a profound artistic allure. The second sentence can be interpreted as either a depiction of the surroundings or as a visualization inspired by the melodious notes of the bamboo flute in the the writer's mind, similar to Zhong Ziqi's thought of high mountains and flowing water when listening to Bo Ya's performance on the *guqin*. Meanwhile, the last two sentences express the enchanting allure of the bamboo flute's sound. This description possesses remarkable qualities, evoking a sense of romance and beauty that captivates people and encourages them to delve deeper into its underlying significance. Of course, the Goddess of Xiaoxiang River possesses distinct characteristics that set her apart. She could not be summoned, but the resonance of the bamboo flute can evoke a response from her. When the sound of a jade pendants ring is heard from the water, she is standing and attentively listening.

塞鸿秋

山行警

无名氏

东边路，西边路，南边路。

五里铺，七里铺，十里铺。

行一步，盼一步，懒一步。

霎时间天也暮，日也暮，云也暮。

斜阳满地铺，回首生烟雾。

兀的不山无数，水无数，情无数。

品读

这支曲写一个山行的旅人落日时分的茫然之思，曲语重叠反复，层层推进，有鲜明的艺术个性。

"东边路西边路南边路，五里铺七里铺十里铺"，仿佛无数旅途印象的骤然涌出。这个人似乎一直都在走路，东边、西边、南边，天下的路几乎都走遍了，到处都是五里铺、七里铺、十里铺，什么地方才是旅途的尽头呢？一步步地在接近又总是伸手难及，而家乡故园也一步步地在远离，真让人心绪难平呀。"行一步盼一步懒一步"，这仿佛已不是具体的旅途，简直就是令人疲累的人生。落日时分，山色分外晴和美丽，回望走过的地方，山山水水已笼入一片暮霭之中，迷迷蒙蒙间，只觉有无数浓浓的旅途情思，正密密匝匝地直袭人心。

Tune: Autumn Swan on Frontier

On My Way in the Mountain

Anonymous

On eastern way, on western way, on southern way,

Five miles away, seven miles away, ten miles away.

I go slow-paced, I stop slow-paced, I look slow-paced.

Suddenly the sky is effaced,

The sun effaced, the clouds effaced.

The earth is paved with departing sunbeams;

Turning my head, I find mist grow as dreams.

Does mist not veil the countless hills and rills?

Does it not hide my sorrow which heart fills?

Literary Appreciation

This song poem depicts the contemplative musings of a mountain traveler during sunset through repetitive language and progressively layered elements, showcasing a unique artistic style.

The sentences "East road, west road, south road, five miles, seven miles, ten miles" indicate a multitude of journeys. The speaker appears to be always walking; they have extensively traveled across various regions of the country in the east, west, and south, and seen so many post stations along their journey. However, where is the final destination of their journey? They are traveling closer to their destination, while farther from their hometown;

159

this circumstance can evoke feelings of unease and restlessness. Then, the sentences "I go slow-paced, I stop slow-paced, I look slow-paced" indicate that the traveler is no longer walking on an actual path, but rather the path of their straining life. As the sun sets, the mountains ahead seem remarkably bright and beautiful. However, when they look back, the mountains and rivers on the roads they have passed are shaded in the twilight, evoking a range of intense emotions experienced throughout the journey, deeply impacting the traveler on an emotional level.

凭阑人

金陵道中

乔吉

瘦马驮诗天一涯，
倦鸟呼愁村数家。
扑头飞柳花，
与人添鬓华。

品读

元人似乎特别擅写天涯漂泊之感，马致远一曲《天净沙·秋思》，倾倒了古今无数读者；乔吉这一曲《凭阑人·金陵道中》，虽不似前者那样"天下谁人不识君"，但也以一种茫然飘零的人生诗趣，使读过它的人记忆深切。

"瘦马驮诗天一涯"一句，艺术意趣最为饱满，不仅让人想到李贺的坎坷命运、奇崛诗思，也让人联想到陆游的"衣上征尘杂酒痕，远游无处不销魂。此身合是诗人未？细雨骑驴入剑门"。乔吉是自许为诗人的，也有着诗人漂泊感伤的沉重。以下三句，都可以视为这种人生的展开与显露。"倦鸟呼愁村数家"，是金陵道中的具体情境，也是诗人随时浮上心头的疲倦惆怅心绪。"扑头飞柳花，与人添鬓华"，鲜活平易的两句话，轻轻一笔，更深地写出了那种迟暮心境，哀而不怨，典雅清丽，确属曲中上品。

Tune: Leaning on Balustrade

On My Way to Jinling

Qiao Ji

Skinny horse carries poems written by me in exhausted,

Tired birds bewail over desolate villages in sight.

Overhead willow down in flight,

Adds to my hair at temples white.

Literary Appreciation

Writers of the Yuan dynasty seem to be exceptionally proficient in capturing the sentiment of wandering the remote corners of the world, as evident by Ma Zhiyuan's *Tune: Sunny Sand Autumn Thoughts*, which has captivated numerous readers throughout ancient and modern times. Qiao Ji's *Tune: Leaning on Balustrade*, while not as renowned as Ma's work, evokes a profound sense of introspection and contemplation on the transient nature of life.

The sentence "Skinny horse carries poems written by me in exhausted" is most artistically expressed, as it not only serves as a poignant reminder of Li He's tumultuous destiny and his exceptional poetic musings, but also evokes associations with Lu You's "clothes are stained with dust and wine, and traveling far and wide is fascinating. Am I also a poet? Riding a donkey into the guard pass in drizzle". Qiao Ji identified himself as a poet, meaning that he possessed the characteristic introspection and emotional depth often associated with those in this creative field, which can be revealed through "Tired birds

162

bewail over desolate villages in sight", an actual situation occurred on Jinling Road and a presentation of Qiao's wearied and melancholic state of mind that arises at any time, and "Overhead willow down in flight, Adds to my hair at temples white", which vividly and straightforwardly capture the profound emotional state that is both melancholic and elegant. The imagery depicted in these portrayals exhibits exceptional quality, positioning it unquestionably at the apex of excellence among song poems.

金字经

吴弘道

这家村醪尽，

那家醅瓮开，

卖了肩头一担柴。

哈！

酒钱怀内揣。

葫芦在，

大家提去来。

品读

　　此曲以第一人称的口吻塑造了一位打柴换酒的樵夫形象，语言生动、活泼欢快，洋溢着劳动生活的快乐和劳动者豪爽健康的生命气息，与晦暗苍白的士大夫生活迥异其趣，表现出作者对农村淳朴生活的由衷向往和热爱。

　　"这家村醪尽，那家醅瓮开"两句，渲染出一种农家生活富足安乐的景象，欢快的气息扑面而来，对打柴的樵夫，这无疑是一种诱惑。"卖了肩头一担柴，哈！酒钱怀内揣"，樵夫卖柴后那一副快活自在、兴冲冲直奔酒肆的样子，活灵活现，如在目前。"葫芦在，大家提去来"，酒已喝足，兴余还在大声招呼着朋友，那一种豪爽劲儿，真叫人痛快。

Tune: Gold Character Classics

Wu Hongdao

There are a little home brewed wine in this family,

There are a new jar of wine be opened in that family.

Sold out the woods of my shoulder,

Fantastic!

I have money to drink!

Wine—gourd is still here,

Everyone enjoys to buy wine with it.

Literary Appreciation

This song poem is written in the first—person perspective, depicting a woodcutter who sells firewood in exchange for wine through vivid and cheerful language, which emanates from a deep sense of joy derived from labor and daily life. The depicted lifestyle stands in stark contrast to the monotonous and lackluster lifestyle of the scholar—officials, effectively conveying the writer's genuine longing and affection for a simple rural lifestyle.

The two sentences, "There are a little home brewed wine in this family, There are a new jar of wine be opened in that family", depict a scene of abundance and joy in a farmhouse, creating a cheerful environment that undoubtedly tempts the woodcutter, who earns a living by selling firewood. Meanwhile, "Sold out the woods of my shoulder, Fantastic! I have money to

165

drink!" vividly paint the woodcutter's expression of happiness and relief, followed by their immediate visit to the wine shop after selling firewood. His joy is further demonstrated in "Wine-gourd is still here, Everyone enjoys to buy wine with it", where even after he fills himself with wine, the woodcutter continues to call for his friends to join him. The depiction of adventurousness in this particular scene effectively evokes a profound sense of delight and elation among the readers.

醉太平

钟嗣成

风流贫最好，

村沙富难交。

拾灰泥补砌了旧砖窑，

开一个教乞儿市学。

裹一顶半新不旧乌纱帽，

穿一领半长不短黄麻罩，

系一条半联不断皂环绦，

做一个穷风月训导。

品读

原作一组三首，此为其三。

钟嗣成此曲，以玩世不恭的姿态，塑造了一个落魄文人的形象，诙谐里包藏着悲辛，游戏中包藏着桀骜，是对当时社会现实的一种大胆嘲弄和挑战。

"风流贫最好，村沙富难交"是主人公对生活的一种认识，也是他所有愤世行为的思想根基，元代社会的不合理，使大多数的才智之士找不到发挥他们才能的机会，对那些粗野、鄙俗的有钱人，他们打心底里看不起，于是便有很多人混迹社会底层，与乞儿、娼妓为伍，在那里寻找一点人生的乐趣和自由。关汉卿宣称自己"是个普天下郎君领袖，盖世界浪子班头"（《南吕·一枝花》），钟嗣成也宣称要"做一个穷风月训导"。

Tune: Drunk in Time of Peace

Zhong Sicheng

It's happy in love with the poor,

It's hard to make friends with the rich.

I would repair an old brick-kiln with clay,

And open a school for beggars by day.

I will put on a black hat half outworn,

And a yellow cloak half torn,

With a disjointed belt ill at ease,

To be a teacher with beggars to enjoy the moon and breeze.

Literary Appreciation

This song poem is the third and last song poem in a collection.

In this song poem, the writer cynically portrayed an image of a destitute scholar. Through a combination of melancholic humor and rebellious undertones, the song poem boldly ridicules and questions the prevailing societal reality of its era.

The speaker's perception of life revolves around the notion that " It's happy in love with the poor; It's hard to make friends with the rich", which has served as the fundamental basis for all their cynical actions. The irrationality of the societal structure of the Yuan dynasty had resulted in a significant obstacle for talents to give full play to their abilities, most of which looked down on rude and vulgar people of wealth. Therefore, many frequent the lower echelons of society, associating themselves with beggars and courtesans, and seek enjoyment and liberation within this particular milieu. In Guan Hanqing's *Tune: A Sprig of Flower*, he proclaimed himself as " a leader of the world, and also a prodigal guy of the world"; similarly, Zhong expressed his intention to "be a poor and romantic disciplinarian".